Tempted by a Vampire

Immortal Hearts of San Francisco

Stephanie
All the best
Susan Griscom

Also by Susan Griscom

The Whisper Cape Trilogy
Whisper Cape
Reflections
A Secret Fate

The Beaumont Brothers Series
Beautifully Wounded
Beautifully Used

The Sectorium Series
A Gypsy's Kiss

Single Titles
Allusive Aftershock

Tempted by a Vampire

Immortal Hearts of San Francisco

Susan Griscom

Tempted by a Vampire is a work of fiction. All of the characters,
organizations, and events portrayed in this novel are either
products of the author's imagination or are used fictitiously.

Amber Glow Books
www.susangriscom.com

Edited by Michael Leah Olson
Cover Design by Susan Griscom
Cover Model: Weston Bouchér
Cover Photos: www.Romancenovelcovers.com
ISBN: 978-1517602239

For Harry

Chapter One

Cian

The city seemed almost too calm for a Saturday night. Something major was about to happen. My bones twitched and I grew antsy as a sentience floated through my mind, warning of change. I was coming off a three-day work-a-thon. We all were. "We all" being the band—my brother Lane, Gage, Elvis, and myself. Work binges were frequent occurrences when we got in these creative moods, but this time, it left me feeling a bit enervated.

"Ari, pull over," I growled with unease at our driver.

"What's up?" Lane frowned from the limo seat across from me.

"I need some air."

"You feeling okay?" he asked before downing a shot of Johnny Walker Black. We always kept a bottle in the limo. The booze helped calm the nerves. No matter how long we'd been doing this, the jitters always showed up.

"Yeah, I just need a bit of refreshing."

Lane smiled. "Be safe, don't get yourself mugged," my brother warned then sat back, chuckling as he downed another shot.

1

"Make it a quickie!" Gage laughed. "We go on in forty minutes."

"Just a quickie," I agreed as I shut the door.

I walked past a small corner store and headed up a hill where rows of townhomes graced each side of the street—each one a different color but with similar architecture. As I roamed the north shore neighborhood, the sound of a cable car bell chimed from another, not-too-distant block.

A door in one of the homes opened. I hung back and waited, watching as a young woman came out of an apartment building. A twenty-something beauty with long, blonde hair and a straight nose set between high cheekbones. Her long, shapely legs extended from a very short, black-and-white-flowered skirt. A large, chartreuse purse swung from her arm. Exactly what I needed to tame the heightened levels of testosterone soaring through my body, tightening my balls. Not to mention sate my need for sustenance. There were plenty of homeless lurking around the city—particularly in the park—that could have done fine, but I didn't go for those. I liked my victuals clean, exactly like this delectable morsel.

I stepped out of the shadows as she came down the steps to the sidewalk. "Excuse me," I said, inching closer. She smiled. *Mmm, a very kissable mouth.*

"Can I help you?"

"Walk with me," I commanded, staring into her wide, brown eyes as I took her palm in mine. She easily capitulated, succumbing to my compulsion, and continued to smile as we strolled hand in hand down the hill as if we were a young couple in love. We turned into an alley a short distance from the home she'd just left.

I didn't kill, and I only took what I needed.

"May I kiss your neck?" I asked, wanting to hear her approval. It made the seduction more enjoyable to me.

"Of course."

I licked at her vein and pressed tiny kisses along the length of her throat. Then I skimmed my hand up along her inner thigh. "May I fuck you?"

"Please."

She'd been easily compelled, affording me great pleasure, the way I liked it. And while part of me felt a little bit guilty because she wasn't fully aware, I knew that she would be equally pleasured. I would care for her as much as I could. Though, it was impossible for me to force something like this on someone unless they secretly already wanted it.

I ripped off the flimsy panties she wore and unfastened my pants, letting them fall to my knees. I didn't relish fucking in alleys, but I didn't have time to take her back to the mansion where I lived with my brother and bandmates.

I plunged into her sweet den of wickedness, thrusting hard. She gasped. My hips drove forward again. She took me in as far as I could go, uttering a pleasured moan. *Perfect.* I didn't believe in tormenting my prey. If anything, I wanted them to enjoy the experience as much as I did.

"This won't hurt," I promised then pierced my fangs into her neck, sinking them deep and letting her sweet nectar flow into my mouth.

She came almost immediately as the titillating sensation of having her blood sucked gently from her vein cast her over the edge.

I didn't want to drain her, nor did I want to hurt her in any way. When I was sure she'd climaxed at least three times, I pumped into her hard and released, letting my essence explode into her as her blood filled me with renewed strength and energy. I stopped sucking and licked the wounds closed with the tip of my tongue.

I tugged my pants up and smoothed her skirt down.

"Thank you," I said.

"You're welcome." She smiled.

I straightened a few strands of her hair that stuck up from where I'd pressed her against the wall. "You won't remember any of this. You will remember spending a wonderful evening with a date. Experiencing the greatest pleasure imaginable. And you will recall that you were very tired and decided to return home early, take a shower, and head to bed." She blinked, the glazed state of compulsion still evident in her eyes.

She yawned. "I feel like I could sleep for days," she mumbled to herself as she headed out of the alley toward the sidewalk in front of her apartment.

I waited until she'd turned the corner and then I strolled out of the alley toward the club where we performed, passing a few small restaurants and bars along the way. I felt a bit better, but I was still on edge.

As I rounded the corner in front of Club Royal, my eyes caught and held the penetrating stare of what had to be a goddess straight from heaven. Through the window of my favorite small, but quaint Italian restaurant, the gaze of a gorgeous and well-toned woman followed me as I walked. She sat with another, sipping a martini. Her unpretentious demeanor was alluring, and my cock twitched, immediately followed by a discontented feeling. I knew that the brief encounter a few moments ago had been nothing more than an aphrodisiac. The temptation to stop and seduce the woman was almost overwhelming, but I didn't have time. The guys would kick my ass if I left them to set up without me.

Chapter Two

Magdalena

Intense, sexy eyes locked with mine as they slipped around the corner of the building along with the hot body of the man they belonged to. I didn't think I'd ever seen anyone so beautiful before.

This was bad news.

San Francisco just might become a fleeting memory of something in my past. If Kellen ever realized what goodies of the male variety lurked around the city, he'd surely insist that I move to Sacramento to be closer to him. We'd decided on six months. I'd move to the city to pursue my career, and he'd move to Sacramento to pursue his. Seeing each other on weekends whenever time allowed. Wouldn't you know, the weekend Vanessa and I decided to move here, Kellen had a charity event to attend for the mayor, leaving us girls to do all the heavy lifting and unpacking.

I sighed, missing him. Wishing he'd been able to get out of the event.

Seeing the gorgeous guy outside had made me feel lonely, wanting. If I knew what was best for me, I'd forgo the drink and head home to unpack the gazillion boxes practically littering every inch of our new apartment.

"Vanessa, really, I think we should go home and get the place put together," I said as I stood.

"We can't leave, Mags." Vanessa tugged my arm and yanked my small, five-foot-two-inch frame back into the chair I'd been sitting on. A very uncomfortable chair I might add. The kind with little hollow squares made of metal and no cushion to soften the seat. I didn't exactly possess the plumpest rear end in the world, and I was positive that the back of my thighs resembled a waffle iron, indented with ugly squares that would take hours to go away. Those wire chairs were murder on thighs, especially while wearing a mini skirt.

"Really, Vanessa, I think we've had enough."

"We can't go home yet. This is our first night in the city. *Home*, here in the city. Doesn't that sound great?" Vanessa hummed out the word "home" as though she'd never had one before. We'd both come from middle-class families in the Bay Area. Vanessa and I had been college roommates at Chico State and had been planning to move to San Francisco ever since our freshman year. Now that we'd graduated and had both managed, by some miracle, to score top-paying jobs in the city—mine in journalism, hers in graphic design—our dream had finally become a reality.

"It sounds wonderful," I agreed wholeheartedly.

"We didn't move to San Francisco so we could sit in our apartment every night. It's only seven-thirty," Vanessa continued.

"No, of course not. I know. It's just been a long day moving all those boxes in and exhaustion has caught up with me. I'm more tired than I thought I would be. I'd love to just go back and put my feet up. Maybe relax and take a long bubble bath in that big, jetted bathtub we have. We're going to be living here. We can come out another night."

"But we're celebrating." She pouted. "And it's Saturday night. Besides, we haven't eaten yet. Plus, I want to go to that club we passed by earlier. The one that has the live band. I was hoping that you'd loosen up a bit after that martini. Why *are* you so uptight anyway? It's not like you. Is it because Kellen didn't want you to move out here?"

Kellen, my boyfriend for the past two years, had found an awesome job in Sacramento working at the mayor's office. Kellen Slade wanted to be a politician. His dream was to be President of the United States. He had high ambitions, to say the least; much higher than my own, which were, in my opinion, a nine point five on a scale of one to ten. But Kellen Slade's aspirations blew the top off the charts, and usually left me gasping for breath. Vanessa was right, though; Kellen had been less than agreeable about me moving to San Francisco. In fact, he'd been downright pissed off, and had threatened to end our relationship. It had taken hours and hours of coaxing with promises that we'd see each other on weekends whenever possible to get him to agree. He'd finally consented to a six-month trial period. He'd move to Sacramento, and I'd move to San Francisco. We'd be a short hour and twenty-seven-minute drive apart on a good day without traffic. "It has nothing to do with Kellen. I'm just tired."

"Well, I'm not going home yet. You can go, but I'm not spending my first Saturday night in the city watching some lame movie on TV. Besides, we got all dressed up tonight."

She was right, we had. She wore her new black dress. It was trimmed with black lace and had an open lace mid-drift. The décolletage dipped way down close to the top of the lace in the middle. She'd even curled her long, pink-tipped blonde hair, and the way it flowed over her shoulders with the tips dipping into the valley between her breasts was so pretty. Super sexy. My dress wasn't quite as risqué, but equally sexy in my opinion. The silver, silky material shimmered and required a strapless demi-bra that boosted the cleavage the dress revealed. It was very form-fitting and hugged my body maybe a little too tightly. Both of our dresses were extremely short, much shorter than I normally felt comfortable in, but I'd bought it anyway at V's insistence. Our dresses had been purchased last week, right after we'd signed the papers for the lease of the apartment, and bought specifically for our first night out in the city.

Vanessa knew I'd cave. What kind of person would I be if I left my best friend alone at a restaurant in San Francisco on our first night living here, to then walk home by herself after a night of drinking and dancing? Too many horrible scenarios came flooding into my mind. Anyone walking home alone after midnight—especially someone who possessed a curvy body like Vanessa's—was sure to be rape bait for some scuzzy pervert.

So, I relented.

"All right, all right. We'll check out the band, but please don't wake me up in the morning before twelve noon. Okay?"

"Deal. Two more dirty martinis," Vanessa said to the waiter as he passed by our table. He nodded with a smile that could melt the snowcaps off Mount Everest. "Extra dirty," she added. "God, he's adorable, isn't he?"

I nodded, but I couldn't get my mind off of the sexy man who'd captured my attention a while ago.

We drank the martinis and giggled through a shared plate of calamari then headed down the street to the club.

On our way, we passed by a sidewalk sign that proclaimed "Psychic Readings" with an arrow pointing to a door.

"I think we need to check this out. Don't you?" V said.

"Oh, I don't know."

"Mags, stop being so…Mags."

"What's that supposed to mean?"

"Nothing. Sometimes you can be too…safe. C'mon, let's live

a little and be adventurous." Her green eyes gleamed with excitement. How could I refuse?

I rolled my eyes. "Okay." What harm could there be? I didn't believe in psychics or even magic. It was probably just some little old lady who needed a few extra bucks to get her through until her next social security check came in, sitting at a round table with a black cloth draped over it. I could help out with that. After all, I had a brand new, top-paying career at Channel Seven News starting on Monday.

Vanessa opened the door. A long, narrow stairway leading up to the second floor was on the left, and another one led down. Another sign, "Madam Fontaine's Psychic Readings – Downstairs" was posted on the wall.

The stairway was quite ominous and creepy. *Very apropos*, I thought to myself as I grabbed Vanessa's hand and let her lead the way. Worn, frayed carpet edged our path as we made our way down the steep, dark steps.

Another small, black and white sign on the door read, "Come In."

Vanessa looked at me and turned the knob. The door creaked as she opened it.

Five seconds later, a woman—nothing like the little old lady who needed some extra cash that I'd pictured—walked into the room. She wore a low-cut top, revealing some awesome tattoos of birds and music. Her dark hair sparkled with trinkets and flowed over bare shoulders. More colorful tattoos decorated each of her arms; some were very pretty. If I had to guess, I'd say she was about thirty-two.

"Welcome, I'm Tessa Fontaine."

Tessa was tall, hot, and beautiful. I suddenly felt very self-conscious of my squatty shortness. That happened a lot whenever I was around tall women. I'd become used to Vanessa, but always seemed to get a little overwhelmed whenever there was more than one tall lady around me at the same time. My high heels didn't provide as much height as I'd like.

"I'm Vanessa, and this is Mags. Maggie." Vanessa shoved me in front of her. I gave her a sarcastic thanks-a-whole-hell-of-a-lot-friend glance and smiled timidly at Madam Fontaine.

Tessa took my hand. "Come with me, Maggie. Or is Maggie short for something else? I will tell you everything you need to know."

"I…uh, I don't need to know anything…" V's hands shoved at my shoulders, coaxing me to follow Tessa, and I tripped over my own two feet. Somehow, I managed to catch myself without flailing uncontrollably and slamming into the psychic's equally tattooed bare back. "And it's just Maggie." We didn't really need to go into all the history surrounding the name Magdalena, or the fact that my parents thought it would be sweet to give their little girl a designation that meant *rare beauty*. Something I'd always thought I had a difficult time living up to.

"Please, sit." Tessa pointed to a chair positioned at a small round table covered with a black, satiny material. At least my ideas of that turned out to be correct.

Madam Fontaine—Tessa—sat across from me, and Vanessa took a seat by the wall behind me.

"Twenty dollars," Tessa said, holding out her hand. I reached into my purse and pulled out one of the three twenty-dollar bills I had in there.

She placed the money in a box behind her and took my hands in hers. "You've never been in love." This was a statement, not a question. I opened my mouth to protest because I'd been in love with Kellen for the past two years. But as I said, I didn't believe in psychics or magic anyway, so I smiled and played along.

"Hmmm…you will live a very long life."

I almost laughed. That sounded like something all psychics

would start with.

"No, wait," she hesitated. "Long, yes, but..." She shook her head.

"What?"

"Someone dark is about to enter your life. You are about to fall," she continued. "Something is going to break. A relationship? Not a loved one. Not a friend," she assured when Vanessa made some sort of gasping sound behind me. "Falling is inevitable, though."

"Falling?"

She shook her head and made a shushing sound. "Falling under."

"Falling under what?" I asked.

"Falling under temptation."

"Temptation of what?" I asked.

"That is all I see. I can't tell you something I don't see."

"What about the dark person who is about to enter her life?" Vanessa asked.

"I lost sight of him. I'm sorry." Tessa shook her head again.

This was ridiculous. She had to be a fake, and I had just given her my twenty dollars.

"What? How could you lose sight? You're just making this up, right?"

"No. I don't make things up. I only tell you what I see. My visions are not always clear, or rather, translatable, but they *are* always true. Do you want me to read yours?" This last statement she addressed to V.

"Why not?" My friend smirked.

Vanessa and I traded seats and Vanessa paid her twenty dollars. Tessa went on to tell her that she too would live a long life, but without the added hesitation the psychic had done with me. Vanessa would have a prosperous career and a happy marriage.

Madam Fontaine had even added two kids into V's fortune. It seemed that Vanessa's life was to be very mundane. Everything I'd ever wanted.

After the disastrous reading that would probably ruin not only my night but also my entire life, we finally resumed our trek down the hill to Club Royal. It seemed the additional martini had given me a second wind, and I was now ready for some fun and music.

"Crap, there's a line. C'mon." V tugged my arm, and we picked up the pace to a slow jog, which was no small feat in four-inch heels. When you were as short as I was, high heels were your best friend, especially when your real best friend was five-eight.

The black wall we stood beside in the line made the street seem dark and somewhat scary. Various etchings of symbols that I didn't recognize graced the side of the wall. I was anxious to get off the street and inside, but at the same time, a little apprehensive about going in at all.

We stood in line for about three minutes when a rather large, muscle-bound guy in a dark sports coat and pants walked up to us. A small, curly wire connected to an earpiece dangled from his left ear.

"You two, come with me," he ordered.

Vanessa and I looked at each other then back at the man.

"It's safe. You've been bumped up to the front of the line."

We followed the guy inside, and he led us to a small round table right in front of the stage.

"Enjoy," he said, as a waiter stood by and Vanessa ordered two more dirty martinis, this time, with extra olives. At this rate, I'd need to switch to water soon or I'd be crawling home.

"How do you like that?" she said. "Front row seats and we didn't have to wait in the line. I love being a woman." She smiled, placing her chin on her fists.

It was dark and warm in the club. I was glad I'd worn the strapless number Vanessa had talked me into wearing. At first, I'd almost forgone the new dress and put on a black cashmere sweater since it was early October, and the nights in San Francisco were chilly. But inside this room, it felt more like a balmy summer evening.

The band hadn't started to play yet, or maybe they were on a break. Conversation buzzed around us as we both took in the scene. I felt a little better about the place as I studied the clientele. Most seemed upscale but young. Twenty to thirtyish. And there were probably three women to every man. Of course, that was typical in these places. Most of the women wore tight, slinky, form-fitting dresses or pants that looked as if they'd poured themselves into them, and the guys were mostly in jeans and nice shirts.

Vanessa and I sipped our drinks a bit slower this time around as we sat in wonderment.

I glanced up to see two small balconies, one on each side of the club. Each balcony sported a small, round table and two chairs. A woman and a man sat at one of them, sipping cocktails, but the other one was empty. "I wonder how you get to sit up there?" I gestured at the empty balcony, not wanting to draw the attention of the couple sitting on the other one and have them notice that I was pointing.

Vanessa followed my finger. She grinned. "Wow, wouldn't that be fantastic? These are good seats, though. Right up front."

"Please, let's not stay too late," I said. "Especially if the band isn't very good."

"Okay. I agree. Nothing worse than sitting at a table by ourselves, listening to crappy music and yawning. However, I don't think we'll be alone much longer."

I noticed Vanessa smile and I followed her gaze toward the bar where a very hot man with dark, curly brown hair hanging below his ears was standing. To my amazement, he was the same gorgeous man I'd locked eyes with outside of the restaurant earlier. He looked over at us and returned the smile.

Before I knew what had happened, he'd pulled a chair up to our table and sat down. "Hello, ladies." He had an English accent. Or was it Australian? "I haven't seen you in here before." Definitely English. He wore jeans—tight ones—and a black button-down shirt.

"We just moved here. This is our first time in this club," Vanessa supplied. But his gaze—he had the most beautiful silver-blue eyes I'd ever seen—stuck with me. I sipped my martini, feeling a bit uncomfortable. Electric. Looking into his eyes was like floating through the clearest part of the ocean with rays of sunshine painting glimmering streaks of light through the water.

"Well, I hope you enjoy the music. I'm Cian Demarco. I'm with the band."

He pronounced his name like key-in. An odd name. Old maybe. I wondered if he spelled it with a Ke or a Ci? I didn't ask though.

Vanessa giggled and said, "I'm Vanessa, and this is Mags."

"Mags?" His eyebrows lifted with the question.

"Mags is short for Magdalena," my flirtatious roommate happily supplied with a broad grin, knowing I hated my given name.

"Maggie," I corrected, and he gave me a delicious smile. All of a sudden, I felt completely horrible about Kellen not being here. I shouldn't have been thinking about how hot this guy was, but the sensations flowing through my blood made my heart palpitate and my thighs throb. There was no denying it; there was something compelling about him. I wondered if "with the band" meant that he was actually one of the musicians, or if he just worked the lights or sound system. Considering he was hanging out here with the customers, drinking, I decided he must be the sound guy. Or maybe the manager. I was sure the band members were backstage preparing or whatever it was they did before a performance.

"Magdalena. Like Mary Magdalene?"

I rolled my eyes, and he chuckled. "A rare beauty, indeed."

My eyes shot to his. Not many people knew that meaning. He nodded slightly, and one side of his mouth curved up. Sexy.

Cian held up his finger to someone across the room. "Ladies, you will have to excuse me. It seems that it is nine o'clock and the show must go on. Stick around. Maybe we can get to know each other a little after the show."

"We'll probably be leaving early," I said, not wanting to lead him on. After all, I did have a boyfriend.

"That would be a shame." He stood, and I watched him disappear into the crowd that had gathered around all the tables behind us.

Chapter Three

Cian

"Cian," my brother whisper-shouted my name rather abruptly from behind me. I turned to face him. Annoyed.

"What?"

"Are you ready, man?" he whispered again.

"Yes." Pivoting to face the audience again, my eyes unconsciously snapped back to the beautiful woman sitting at the table in front of me.

"Well, you sure the hell aren't acting like it," he said, now standing too close beside me. "We've started the set three times, waiting for you to begin singing."

"Uh. Sorry, Lane. Yeah, let's go," I said, tearing my eyes away from her—the raven-haired beauty, Magdalena. Her name flowed through my mind like sweet classical music on a summer breeze with small, graceful birds floating behind it. I tried to focus on the lights in the back of the room, but my eyes always snapped back to hers, as if pulled by some magnetic force.

I had to admit, it had been a long time since my eyes had had the pleasure of drinking in such a lovely creature. I wondered if those perfect light brown streaks in her hair were natural. I couldn't tell, but my fingers ached to run through the strands. I wanted to caress her neck. And she smelled fucking delicious. My fangs involuntarily elongated, and I had to keep my mouth shut so they wouldn't show as my cock tightened in my pants at the thought of lying with her. When the music started again, I couldn't move. Singing seemed impossible.

"Cian." My brother stood beside me again. "Are you all right?"

I turned toward him. "I need a minute."

"Jesus. Look at you." He leaned closer to my ear. "Your fangs are showing and your eyes are silver. Go backstage for a few minutes. We'll cover for you. Come back when you've gotten yourself under control."

I placed my guitar down, resting it against the stand on the floor and walked off stage. I heard boos and some other derogatory remarks as I headed behind the curtain. I grabbed the bottle of scotch we always kept back there and poured myself a shot. As I let the burn coat my throat, I heard Lane address the audience.

"No worries, ladies. My brother will be right back. I promise. It seems Cian needs to find his voice. It may have become lodged somewhere in his pants." He laughed, and everyone laughed with him. "In the meantime, we'll start with this little number I'm sure you all know."

Great gods of Eros! Now everyone knew I had a hard-on. I supposed that was better than having them see my fangs and eye color change to glowing, silver-rimmed circles. I'd seen beautiful women before, but none of them had ever affected me like this one did.

Fuck me. Her scent was intoxicating. The mentation surrounding what her blood would taste like on my tongue had my libido skyrocketing and clouded everything in my head.

It was coincidence that I'd happened to walk outside the club

17

to look at the line of people waiting to enter. I'd never done that before, but something had tugged at my gut to be out there. When I saw Magdalena—the same strikingly gorgeous goddess I'd seen sitting at that small restaurant—standing in line with her friend, I'd told Ari, our human friend and confidant, to bring them inside to the front table. After they'd been seated, I couldn't stay away. I had to go introduce myself. Except now, I was standing backstage with a fucking hard-on.

The band played *Time*, a Pink Floyd number from the nineteen seventies that we usually performed toward the end of the night. It was one that didn't require me to sing along, so they could manage it without me. Plus, it was a long song. As the tune played out and got close to the end, my blood cooled, though I still had a semi-hard-on. I paced to the end of the hall and back again.

Gods, the way her soft, brown curls flowed into the center of her cleavage made me want to caress the silky strands between my fingers. I wanted to pull them to my lips so I could revel in the texture and smell of the smooth tendrils as they glided across my mouth. I poured another shot glass full of scotch and downed it. Alcohol usually calmed me, dulled some urges, but I feared that there might not be enough whiskey in the bottle—hell, the world— to settle me tonight.

My vampirism was no secret to my brother. In fact, we'd both been cursed with the immortal disease at the same time. Well, within a few minutes of each other, anyway. We'd been traveling together on a ship from London when a beautiful, sexy creature had befriended us. We'd sat around one night, drinking and flirting, when she decided she wanted to experience her first ménage and had asked us to be her partners. We'd both shrugged our shoulders as if it were no big deal and happily obliged. We never turned down a beautiful woman's proposition for sex, even if we had to share. The rest of the evening was somewhat fuzzy, though. I remember going first, and I do remember enjoying myself. Immensely. After several hours of uninhibited sexual activities, we'd all fallen asleep. When Lane and I had awakened in the morning, she was nowhere to be found. Apparently, two days had passed. When we came to, my brother and I had an insatiable appetite for blood and an extreme distaste for daylight, to the point of feeling unusually lethargic whenever we ventured into it. It didn't take long to understand what we'd become. Legends and fables aside, we quickly became aware, as the plight of our survival became the only thing we could focus on. We managed to obtain enough blood from the other passengers to survive the trip across the ocean, and only killed four or five of them. We were careful to pick the ones who seemed to be alone so that no one would miss them. We kept them hidden with us below, taking only enough blood to get us through the nights until we eventually drained them dry. Then we disposed of their bodies overboard. We hated killing, and were disgusted with ourselves, loathing what we'd become. Soon after arriving in New York, and realizing and perfecting our compulsion abilities, we made a pact never to kill again unless it was absolutely necessary. From then on, we only took enough to survive, never killing. Covering our tracks by compelling our victims—though these days, I preferred to refer to them as lovers—and using the healing saliva from our tongues on the marks our fangs made in their necks. Over the years, we'd lived in various states across the country, finally ending up in California, at the heart of San Francisco. We knew we could survive, and now, for the past two hundred years, we'd been able to contain our bloodlust and keep it to a manageable level where we weren't killing randomly in the streets.

Until tonight.

I burned for Magdalena like I'd never burned for another. I didn't want to harm her. No. I did want to devour her blood to a point of complete and utter satiated bliss, though. We're talking possibly comatose. And I knew that was wrong on so many levels.

One, if I put her into a coma from too much blood loss, I'd only be able to have her once. Two, if I killed her, I'd definitely only be able to have her once. And three, I'd never, *ever* be able to just have her once.

I knew nothing about her except the way she made me feel, but I needed to know everything about her. Some force inside me needed to touch every inch of her skin, to caress each breast as if they were the first ones I'd ever had beneath my palms. I ached to kiss and taste the vein that pulsed down the side of her lovely throat.

There was no way I could have her, not even a sample taste, because…well, because then I knew I'd want to take and take and take until there was no more.

What was it about her that held me entranced?

I took another drink of scotch and entered the restroom. Passing the faceless mirror, I cursed, wishing I could examine myself in the glass before heading back out to the stage.

My eyes still felt deluged with the silver ring around them, but the sensation seemed to be fading some. I took a leak; that helped my boner, and upon blinking a few times, the awareness of the silver in my eyes grew less and less intense. I slid my tongue over my teeth. My fangs had retracted, as well. Somehow, I'd managed to pull myself together. As I left the head, I had a fleeting thought that maybe she would be gone. The idea overwhelmed me with both relief and fear. Relief that I'd be able to perform, fear that if she had left, I might not ever see her again.

Chapter Four

Magdalena

"God, is he sexy or what?" Vanessa said.

"Huh?"

"The brother with the other guitar, the one with the nicely trimmed growth on his face who'd whispered something to Cian before he left the stage."

"Oh, yeah. He is." My mind was still spinning from the fact that Cian was the band's lead singer. And the way his eyes had held mine non-stop from the moment he'd walked on stage, as if we'd both been in some weird trance.

"Did you notice the way Cian stared at you? Wow. Very intense. And to think he had to leave the stage because he had a hard-on." She laughed.

"I believe his brother was talking about his voice." I rubbed my finger around the rim of my glass, a nervous habit I had with cocktails whenever I felt uncomfortable in social settings.

"Don't be naïve. Everyone knew the meaning."

"I'm sure he was joking about that."

She shook her head. "Maybe, but it was damn funny."

"More creepy than funny." I fidgeted uncomfortably in my

chair, wishing she hadn't noticed any of that.

"You should be flattered."

"Flattered because the guy couldn't contain himself as he stared at me? It was definitely creepy, and I do have a boyfriend, remember?"

"Yeah, you keep telling yourself that. And I think Cian is sexy as hell. Mags, the man is hot, and he obviously has it bad for you. Besides, Kellen lives in Sacramento and you live here."

"Kellen's only an hour and a half away. And this guy? He doesn't even know me."

"Sac is very far away when you're Kellen Slade. I give him three days before he's prowling around in Old Sac, looking for someone to slip his dick into."

I sighed. "Kellen loves me; he'd never cheat on me." I lied about that because he already had. Two months ago, when Vanessa and I had taken a weeklong trip to a Las Vegas book signing, he'd gone to a frat party and hooked up with Caroline Snyder's cousin who'd been visiting. I'd found out about the affair when she'd called Kellen's phone. He'd asked me to grab the call for him while he'd been in the other room getting us some wine. He'd been surprised to see her name on the display when I'd handed him the phone, but he took the call anyway and then tried to talk his way out of how he knew her after he'd hung up. I finally got him to admit that he'd slept with her.

But Vanessa didn't know about that. I'd never told anyone after I found out. It was too humiliating. I'd almost left him then, but he'd been so apologetic and sincere about never straying again. I'd believed him because I loved him.

"What about Las Vegas?" she asked, and my eyes snapped to hers.

"What about it?"

"He cheated on you when we went to Las Vegas."

"How...do you know about that?"

"Everybody knows. Mags, when are you going to come to your senses and leave that guy? He is slime. A politician. Can't trust him."

"A wannabe politician," I corrected and finished the last of my martini.

"Exactly. That's worse. He has a lot of ground to cover."

"Are you insinuating that he'd sleep his way to the top?"

"I wouldn't put it past him."

"Geesh, Vanessa. I had no idea you hated Kellen so much."

"I don't hate him. I just don't like the way he treats you, and I don't trust him."

Just then, the waiter set two more drinks down on the table in front of us. Vanessa and I glanced at each other. "Did you order these?" I asked.

"No. You didn't?"

I shook my head and we both looked up at the stage. Cian was back and strapping on his guitar. He briefly glanced our way, grinned, and winked before looking back at his brother. Two seconds later, they started playing.

"He winked," Vanessa said.

"He did, didn't he? Do you think he ordered these?"

"Who else?" she said as we both looked around the dark, crowded club. No one stood out or looked as if they wanted to take responsibility for the drinks.

I looked back at the stage just as Cian brought the microphone to his lips. Resting my chin on my fists, I watched him sing *People Are Strange* by the Doors in a deep, arousing baritone. He had an amazing voice. So smooth. Sexy. Everything about him was sexy. The way he stood, strumming the chords, closing his eyes gently, singing as he held the mic in his hand when he wasn't playing the guitar. He didn't look at me once while he sang, though. I began to wonder if maybe he hadn't sent the drinks, and if, just maybe,

Vanessa and I had both imagined the intensity of his stare earlier.

The band began another number and a guy tapped Vanessa on the shoulder. "Care to dance?" he asked. Vanessa turned to me. "You mind?"

"No. Of course, not."

Two seconds later, she was on her feet, jiggling her bottom on the dance floor. The band played for about forty-five minutes, and Vanessa and her new admirer stayed out on the floor the entire time.

"Thank you!" Cian shouted into the microphone. "We're the Lost Boys of San Francisco and we'll be right back after a short break."

My eyes shot to the stage. *The Lost Boys*? Why would they name themselves after an eighties cult horror movie? I inhaled and braced myself for Cian's all-powerful presence at our table. But he didn't come by. In fact, none of the band members came out into the club.

Vanessa came back to the table, laughing with the guy she'd been dancing with. I'd lost track of her while the band had been playing, my thoughts on Cian, dominating every single one of my brain cells. Vanessa had apparently had more to drink because she seemed a bit wobblier than she'd been an hour ago.

"This is Tanner," she giggled and then plopped down into the chair.

"Nice to meet you," he said, and I smiled politely as he sat in the chair next to Vanessa.

A waiter came by our table, carrying a tray in her hands. "Your drinks are on the house tonight, would you like a refill?"

I felt my eyes widen, and Vanessa gasped.

"Sure," Vanessa said.

"Could I have a glass of water, please?" I asked.

"Absolutely. I'll be right back."

"Free drinks? I love San Francisco!" Vanessa crooned.

A few minutes later, the waiter was back with two more martinis, a beer for Tanner, and a glass of water for me.

"These drinks might be free," I said, "but I need to pace myself. My legs are already numb."

Vanessa laughed. "Mine, too. But at least we can sleep in tomorrow. Dancing helps, you should get out there."

"Well, no one has asked me," I admitted with a bit of chagrin at the realization.

Just then, the Lost Boys were back on stage. Vanessa and Tanner went back to dance some more, and I was left once again with my own mentations. I'd thought somebody would come by and try to lure me out to the floor so that I could make a fool of myself. Dancing wasn't exactly my strong point, so it was just as well that no one bothered with me. But still, it was a bit disheartening to think that I was undesirable. I sat alone for maybe another half an hour, and every once in a while I glanced around the room, wondering why no one ever approached me or even seemed to notice me for that matter. Not once. The entire night. Just as I had that epiphany, Cian pulled a stool to the center of the stage and sat on it. He strummed a single chord on his guitar, and then there was silence.

"This will be our last song of the evening. It's one Lane and I wrote a few years ago, I think it was even on the radio for a short time. I'd like to dedicate it to a rare beauty, Magdalena."

My stomach tingled at the wonderful way my name sounded flowing smoothly from his full lips. Sexy did not even come close to what he was. I had to wonder why he seemed so...so obsessed with me. He didn't know me, and we'd hardly even talked before he'd gone on stage to play. I had to admit, though; the pulls and urges I'd been feeling all night were overwhelming.

I just about swallowed my tongue when Cian began to sing.

As if he knew my thoughts, his eyes locked on mine again as

he crooned out the lyrics to my favorite song. The words were forever etched into the frontal lobes of my mind. I'd played it over and over for several months right after my parents passed away. Cian was singing right to me, as if he knew the song meant something to me.

"Come hold my hand,
I want to feel your life,
Alongside me in this lonely land.
Touching you, feeling you in my life,
In my soul,
In my veins.

Be with me tonight.
Be with me tonight.
We may only have tonight so,
Be with me tonight.

Come hold my hand,
I can't make it in this life,
Without you in my plan.
Touching you, feeling you in my life,
In my soul,
In my veins.

Be with me tonight.
Be with me tonight.
We may only have tonight so,
Be with me tonight.

Come and hold my hand,
I've been too long in this life without you
I need you to help me through all that this life demands

Touching you, feeling you in my life,
In my soul,
In my veins.

Be with me tonight.
Be with me tonight.
We may only have tonight so,
Be with me tonight.

I was frozen in my seat, as Cian's hand extended out toward me and stayed there for a few seconds. I couldn't move a muscle. He held my gaze throughout the entire song.

When the song ended, the crowd exploded with cheers.

"Thank you!" Cian said into the microphone. "Again, we're the Lost Boys of San Francisco, and we're here every Saturday night to entertain you."

Clapping and the buzzing sound of voices ensued as all the band members left the stage.

"We should get home," I said to Vanessa as she and Tanner came swerving back to the table.

"We can't leave yet. He said we should stick around. Remember?"

"I do, but I also have a boyfriend. *Remember?*"

"Oh yeah, that slimeball in Sacramento."

"What slimeball in Sacramento?" Cian asked, standing behind Vanessa before he took a seat in the chair he'd sat in before, the one right next to me. "Maybe I can be of some assistance?"

"No, he's not a slimeball," I said, defending my boyfriend to this stranger.

"Depends on your definition," Vanessa said.

Cian chuckled. "I believe you ladies are having somewhat of a disagreement. Is this someone important to you, Magdalena?

Someone I should be concerned about?"

I stared at him a moment. That was a strange way to put things. As if I belonged to him.

"He's my boyfriend," I said, knowing I would be killing any chances of getting to know Cian. But I also knew that I loved Kellen, and getting to know Cian would be a huge mistake.

"Your boyfriend, huh?"

I nodded.

"I could ask why he's not with you, but I think the better question is, why does your friend here..." he said, gesturing with his hand toward V.

"Vanessa," she said and gave him her best smile.

He flashed that killer grin back at her then returned his attention to me. "Why does your friend, Vanessa, think your boyfriend is a slimeball?"

"He's not. He just...sometimes..."

"Forgets he has a girlfriend," Vanessa finished for me. "So, half the time, he *is* a slimeball."

I hoped Vanessa could feel the daggers my eyes were shooting at her. She was not being fair to Kellen. At all. And definitely not helping with this tempting pull I felt toward Cian or his apparent attraction to me.

"What's up, bro. Hello, ladies. Hey, Tanner." The guy who I guessed was Cian's brother sat down and joined us at our table, too. "I'm Lane, Cian's brother."

"This is Vanessa and Magdalena," Cian supplied.

"Maggie," I quickly suggested, but wasn't sure why since I adored the way Cian pronounced my name.

"Magdalena has a boyfriend," Cian continued, completely ignoring my prompt. It was clear he enjoyed using my given name. "But I'm not sure about Vanessa."

She shook her head. "Single."

"Not tonight," Tanner supplied hastily.

"Nice to meet you," Lane flashed Vanessa that same sexy smile Cian had. Now I knew we were in trouble. Trouble in the form of two undeniably gorgeous and sexy musicians, and one hot guy by the name of Tanner.

"We're trying to establish whether or not Magdalena's boyfriend is a whole slimeball or just a half of one."

"He's not a slimeball at all." I had to laugh. Here I was, defending my boyfriend, who *had* cheated on me, to these two beautiful men, wishing the entire time that I didn't even have a boyfriend. What was wrong with me?

"Well, one of you is right and one of you is wrong. A man who forgets he has a girlfriend doesn't sound like a very good boyfriend. In fact, he sounds more like the slimeball Vanessa is talking about, wouldn't you agree, Lane?"

"Absolutely."

A waiter came over, carrying a tray with five shot glasses filled with something gold. I wasn't quite sure I wanted to know what it was.

"Shots, ladies?" Lane said, passing a glass to each of us.

"Oh, no. Thank you, though," I said.

"You sure?" Cian asked.

"Yes, positive. I believe I've reached my limit. One more drink and I'll be sleeping under this table."

Cian leaned in close to my ear. His breath warm and intoxicating. "I can fix that," he whispered.

"What? No. I don't do drugs."

"Not drugs." He gently tugged my chin with his finger so that my eyes stared squarely into his gorgeous, silver-tinted blue ones. "You're beautiful, Magdalena." He spoke softly, his whispered breath warm and sweet and so close to my lips.

"Yes," I whispered back, believing he spoke the truth.

His eyes were magnificent, beautiful. I'd never seen eyes like his before. I gazed into them, unabashedly. Without thoughts of guilt or deceit that Kellen might be upset about this. Only the beauty of Cian's eyes, their mesmerizing color, and the sound of his voice engaged the functioning parts of my mind.

"You haven't had very much alcohol to drink tonight, have you Magdalena?"

"No, I haven't had much alcohol tonight," I found myself repeating, believing it was true as everything became clear in my head and the room stopped spinning.

"You haven't had enough alcohol tonight to have much of an effect on you. You are completely sober."

"Yes. I am sober." I couldn't stop looking at him. I didn't want to turn away.

With our eyes still locked, his hand lifted mine, and his soft lips skimmed over my fingers. He turned my hand over and his eyes lowered. My eyes trailed his as the tantalizing pressure of his thumb registered where it gently rubbed tiny circles in the center of my palm.

My breath hitched, and I found myself licking my lips. I looked back into his eyes. "There. Now you can drink more," he said, drawing his hand away.

I glanced over at Vanessa with a very clear mind and the fuzzy slurred feeling in my brain completely gone. All except for the heavy temptation of Cian, and the desire to be touched by him again.

"How do you feel, Magdalena?" Cian asked.

"I...I feel fine. Awake." I looked at him.

"Do you remember being a bit tipsy?" His smile was infectious.

"Yes," I grinned.

"But now you're sober?"

"Yes. Completely. How did you do that? Was that some form of hypnosis or something?" I asked.

"Yes, exactly," Cian said.

"You're a hypnotist?"

He shrugged. "We dabble, my brother and I. Amateurs at best."

"I bet you come in pretty handy at parties." I laughed, but I had a weird feeling about the whole experience. Something wasn't right. I just didn't buy into the whole hypnosis theory, but every time I gazed into Cian's eyes, my entire body tingled. I could actually feel the veins in my body throb and pulse with desire for him. Whenever he held my gaze with his, I became aware of only him. It was uncontrollable.

"It's a given. Now, how about these shots?" Cian suggested. We all drank the contents down. It was rather yummy.

"That was good," Vanessa said.

"Just a little thank you for sticking around," Cian said.

Something across the room must have grabbed Lane's attention. He nodded and placed his glass down on the table. "As much as I hate to leave this little party, I have some business to take care of." He stood. "Ladies, I hope to see you again sometime," he said directly to Vanessa then scooted his chair out and walked away.

Cian frowned and watched Lane as he hurried across the room.

"Is everything okay?" I asked.

"Yes. My brother would have liked to stay, but he does have a…"

"A girlfriend?" Vanessa's sigh dripped with disappointment, even though she clung onto Tanner's arm—another attractive man. The club seemed to be brimming with them all of a sudden. But Tanner didn't hold a candle to Lane or Cian, and I knew she wanted to get to know Lane. He was just as hot as Cian, which brought me to the question of what the hell I was doing? I had no right to sit there with him when I had a boyfriend. I knew Kellen wouldn't like it.

"He has...an obligation," Cian said to Vanessa, making whatever commitment Lane had sound much like a forced relationship.

"C'mon, let's go dance." Tanner took Vanessa's hand as music played by a deejay boomed throughout the club.

"Would you like to dance, Magdalena?" Cian asked.

"Um...no. Thank you."

"Ah, is that slimeball boyfriend preventing you from dancing with me?"

I laughed. "No. I'm just a horrible dancer."

"You can't be that bad. Especially in my arms."

Wow, had he just said that? *In his arms?*

Every muscle and bone in my body said: *go dance with him. Let him hold you. Let him hold you until the sun comes up and then some more.* God, I was pathetic. Being away from Kellen obviously made me lonely.

"Come with me." He stood, extending his hand. The temptation was too strong to resist, and I couldn't help but smile. When I placed my hand in his, goose bumps skated up my arm as the thrill of his touch excited me.

Chapter Five

Cian

I would never have been able to stay up on stage if I'd allowed anyone to approach Magdalena for a dance. It had been easy to put out a compulsion demand to all the male assholes in the room to stay away from her. She was mine. At least for tonight.

I led the beautiful Magdalena by the hand to the middle of the dance floor. Her grasp was soft in mine. I felt her shiver when our skin connected. Cold or excitement, I wasn't entirely sure. I decided to go with the latter, and pulled her in close, feeling her heart beat against my chest. Her pulse beckoned to me.

Thump.

Thump.

Thump.

I feared I might not have control over the annoying animalistic behavior every vampire struggled to overcome. Feeding until there was no more.

"Your band is good," she whispered as we weaved our way through couples, swaying together on the dance floor. "And you have a great voice."

"Thanks," I said and reached up to run my finger through the long strands of her hair. I couldn't help myself.

She stopped dancing suddenly, and I worried that I had done something offensive.

"Is everything all right?" I asked.

"Yes…um, no. I should go home. Please, which way is the ladies' room?"

"I'm sorry. Of course, it's this way," I said, leading her to the restroom, fighting the temptation to compel her into staying with me. I didn't want to force this lovely creature to do anything she didn't want to do. I needed her whole and of sound mind, and so, I resolved myself to the knowledge that this seduction would take time. I'd need time to earn her trust. To get her to believe that I would never hurt her. "I'll wait for you out here," I assured her as I held the entrance open for her.

She nodded, and the door closed. I exhaled the breath I'd unconsciously been holding as we'd walked through the club. My lungs now burning without her presence beside me, I didn't understand the pressure in my chest as the sound of my immortal heart reverberated through my ears.

A few minutes later, she emerged, more beautiful than before. Though I knew nothing had changed with her, only my perception of her.

Her infectious smile rendered me lightheaded. I took her hand in mine once again, but now that didn't seem nearly enough as the beat of her pulse soared through my mind, urging, teasing. An uncontrollable need had me pinning her up against the wall. I positioned my body up against hers, pressing myself against her, holding her still. She didn't resist. I didn't compel her to acquiesce. The last thing I wanted was for her desire for me to be forced. I wanted her to be with me because she wanted to be. But that idiot, so-called slimeball of a boyfriend she kept feeling guilty about—if the look on her face were any indication—continued to invade her mind, giving her doubts about what she was doing with me.

"Magdalena, you're so beautiful. Do you know that?" I whispered against her ear, feeling the tug of her pulse as my lips skimmed down the side of her neck, the vein that I desperately wanted to taste calling to me. Just taste. I would never hurt her, but she was so intoxicating.

"I should go," she breathed into my neck as I pressed my lips gently against her vein.

"If you must," I mumbled, not in the least believing my own words.

"You're difficult to walk away from," she breathed.

"I think I like hearing you say that."

"Unfortunately…"

"You have a slimeball of a boyfriend who cheats on you, and you feel the need to be loyal to him," I said in a rather cynical tone. I instantly regretted it.

She sighed. "He only cheated once."

"Once was not enough?" I asked, unable to lessen the amazement in my voice. How was it possible for a beautiful woman to put up with someone so disloyal?

She sighed again.

"You do that a lot."

"What?"

"Sigh."

She did it again and laughed.

"See?"

"I guess I do that when I'm frustrated."

"So, I frustrate you?"

"You might say that."

"I'm not going to pretend that I'm not interested in getting to know you better. I think, if you stay, you'll learn that I might have more to offer than that boyfriend of yours." As difficult as it was, I'd been trying very hard not to read her thoughts. For some reason, invading that part of her, when I felt it was perfectly acceptable for me to do it with anyone else, seemed wrong.

"Is that so?" Her eyelashes fluttered open as she looked up at me, revealing her beautiful blue eyes full of...desire?

"Yes."

"You certainly are sure of yourself."

"I have nothing to lose, Maggie."

"Now it's Maggie?"

"I'm sorry?"

"Well, I was just getting used to the way my real name sounds when you say it."

"Ah. Well, then, I will try to make a conscious effort to call you Magdalena."

"You are a temptation."

"Whatever it takes, Mags."

"Now you're just being mean." She laughed. "Your charm, or your lack of charm, whichever one you use, isn't going to make me stay."

"Do you want to leave?"

"Not really. But I need to."

I pressed my lips briefly against hers, just to see what would happen. As I guessed, she didn't resist. "You do have a choice, Magdalena. Come." I took her hand in mine. "One more dance, then you can leave. And even though you'll be breaking my heart, I'll even pay for your cab home."

She followed me to the dance floor, and I took her in my arms. As I held her close, inhaling her intoxicating smell, she whispered in my ear. "Cian, I wish I could stay. I really do."

"Shhh. No talk of leaving. Let's just enjoy the moment we have together."

When the song ended, I took Magdalena's hand and walked her through the hallway that led to the outside. It was dark and I couldn't resist one last shot at exploring her luscious body. I stopped and turned her to face me. I stepped closer, pinning her gently against the wall, and covered her lips with mine. This kiss was much different than the brief skimming I'd allowed myself earlier.

This kiss held all the allure I wanted her to feel, along with the promise of what could be if she only allowed herself the pleasure.

The cleavage protruding from the top of her dress left me weak in the knees, and my lips found their way to that spot as if they'd been possessed. I kissed the tops of her breasts, and she kissed my neck right below my ear. My fingers ached to touch the skin beneath her silver dress, and I moved to do just that. I found her thigh soft and silky. Almost as silky as the material she wore. My fingers inched up her thigh, massaging gently. I waited for her to stop me. I could have compelled her to let me do whatever I wanted to, but this woman was different. I wanted *her* to want it. To want *me*. When she didn't stop me, I skimmed my forefinger along the edge of her panties and slipped it between her thighs, finding her oh so gloriously wet. My gods, she was stunningly beautiful.

My cock stiffened, a prisoner locked behind a zipper of steel.

"Cian," she breathed against my neck, and I silenced her with my mouth, exploring every inch of hers, tasting, taking what she seemed so willing to give me as my finger teased the soft skin of her thigh just outside of her very wet undergarment. "I need to go." The dreaded words flowed from her swollen lips like poison to my soul, and I had to fight the too-easy urge to compel her to stay.

Chapter Six

Magdalena

The loud sound of birds chirping, as well as the sun beaming in through my new bedroom window, had me pulling my pillow over my head, begging for just a few more minutes of sleep. Coming in at three in the morning had left me a bit drained. Normally, I would have welcomed the sweet chirps and the thought of another new day, especially now that I didn't have to worry about test scores and whether or not I had enough units to graduate. Landing this job with the network was a godsend, and one that I would not take for granted.

I rolled over, removing the pillow from my head. The birds had quieted down, and with the sun now behind my back, I slowly opened my eyes and stared at the bare wall across from my bed. My new bed, my new wall, my new room. My first morning in our new apartment. I briefly squeezed my eyes shut, remembering the club last night. Cian. I had almost given in to him. I had almost cheated on Kellen. God, how could I? Could I be that easily swayed by the wiles of another man just because he was gorgeous? There was something about Cian, though. The lure had been so strong. I'd never been tempted by a man that way before. Of course, I'd never put myself in a position to be tempted like that.

Not until last night.

When Cian had led me into the hallway last night after dancing so close together, I'd felt as if I'd lost all sense of right and wrong. By all rights, *Faithfully* by Journey should have made me want and miss Kellen. But in the heat of the moment, I'd wanted Cian and everything he had to offer. I had no clue what that could be, except pleasure. The strong temptation overwhelmed me. When his lips had been on my neck, I'd wanted to put mine on his. I'd wanted his mouth on mine. I'd so wanted to taste the sweetness of what I thought his tongue would deliver. Experiencing the tenderness of his touch on my skin had almost left me helpless as his fingers skimmed along my waist. His breath against my neck was intoxicating. Where had he been all my life? The two years I'd spent with Kellen now seemed wasted. Did I love Kellen? I had at one time. I must love Kellen, or I wouldn't have stopped Cian when I had. Cian made me feel special, as if I were the only woman he ever wanted to be with. I fought hard to think of a moment in our relationship when Kellen had made me feel that way. My mind went blank. I couldn't think of a single moment in the entire two years we'd been together where I'd felt like I was the only woman Kellen wanted. I knew he had wandering eyes, and he'd had that one-night stand with that woman. But he'd sworn after that that he'd never mess around again, saying it had only been that once, and he'd just been so lonely without me. He'd said he loved me, and I believed him.

Thinking about Kellen made me a bit homesick for him. I reached for my phone on my nightstand. The time on the screen read 10:58 a.m. Wow. I'd slept late. I wondered if Vanessa was up. Oh, God. Had she even come home? I'd let Cian put me in a cab after trying to coax Vanessa out of the club, but she'd been having so much fun with Tanner that she didn't want to leave, and Tanner had promised to bring her home. Cian had assured me that she would be fine with Tanner.

I threw off my heavy coverlet and hurried to Vanessa's room, curious to see if she was there. Hoping she was, her door slightly ajar, I peeked into her room. I let out a sigh of relief, squelching all the horrible thoughts of her lying dead in a ditch somewhere. There she was, on her side, her pink, silk sheets tucked up to her chin and fisted in her hands as she slept snuggled with them. She looked so sweet and innocent. Though, I knew better.

Vanessa always wanted something, or in this case someone, she couldn't have. At least not at that very moment. She'd had the full attention of a very nice guy, but last night, she hadn't been after nice. I knew she'd had her eyes set on Lane. Lane was everything Vanessa usually fell for. He had that rock star, bad boy persona, and I knew she'd practically been foaming at the mouth to mesh her lips with his. Though Tanner was a great looking guy and all, I knew she'd wanted to hang around to see if Lane would return from whatever obligation Cian had said he had. That had been a strange way to put things. Clearly the guy had been preoccupied, was possibly in a relationship, but to call it an "obligation" didn't sound like a normal or willing type of commitment. Since Vanessa had come home, Lane must not have returned.

Speaking of commitments, I thought I'd better give Kellen a call. I went back to my room, hopped back into bed, and scrunched the covers up to my chest. San Francisco mornings were a bit nippy. Something I hoped to get used to. I snatched my phone off the nightstand. After scrolling through my contacts and finding the adorable picture of him wearing his Giant's cap, I tapped on his number. He answered on the third ring.

"Hello?" a female voice crooned into the phone.

I sat up, stunned silent.

"Hello?" she said again, and I heard her sigh in annoyance. "If you're looking for Kellen, he's in the shower."

Quickly pressing the disconnect button, I stared at my phone, not quite comprehending what had just happened.

I rubbed my hand over my face and stared at my phone again. Kellen's cool, adorable picture stared back at me. Mocking. Kellen was cheating on me. Again.

I hadn't even been gone for a full twenty-four hours, and he already had some...some bimbo answering his phone.

"What's up?" A groggy Vanessa yawned and slipped under the covers beside me. "Man, it is freezing. Maybe we should turn the heater on."

"I'm not cold, at least not anymore," I grumbled.

"No?" She tipped the phone in my hands toward her. "Kellen making you hot?"

"Yeah, but not in a good way. Some woman just answered his phone."

"Fuck! What a creep," she groaned and slid almost completely under the covers so that the only parts of her that showed were her eyes and forehead. Then she turned toward me and lowered the blanket a bit to reveal her mouth. "See? Kellen is a slimeball, just like I said. Mags, you're too good for him. Kellen has never treated you like a boyfriend is supposed to treat his lady. Boyfriends are supposed to respect you, bring you flowers, worship you, and show you how much they enjoy being with you by the way they treat you and talk to you. Kellen has never done any of those things."

It was hard hearing that from Vanessa. I wanted to cry, but I couldn't. The more I thought about it, Kellen always did seem to go out of his way to make everything about him and not me.

There was a part of me that wanted a relationship with Kellen, but another that knew he'd never been right for me. And I had to think that maybe I was more in love with the idea of a relationship than I was with Kellen.

"I know. It's over." There I'd said it, weakly, but at least it was out. Except I felt a bit like a failure to all women for allowing Kellen to manipulate me for the past two years.

"You met someone last night who seemed to be totally into you and he *did* do most of those things I mentioned. Already. I saw it. Kellen has never acted like Cian did last night. Never. You know I'm right."

I bit my bottom lip and sniffed in the non-existent tear that I'd tried so hard to conjure. If I cared so much for Kellen, why couldn't I shed a single tear for him? I was mad as hell, but not sad. Sorry I'd wasted two years of my life, but not upset it was over. "You know what?" I asked.

"What?"

"I think I feel a bit of relief that it's over. I'm glad he cheated on me. Now I don't need to feel guilty about pursuing my own dreams." To think I'd given up an opportunity to get to know Cian last night, worrying about Kellen, when he was cheating on me anyway. Yeah, I was more than a bit relieved. I was beyond relieved. I was pissed. I could hardly wait to tell him it was over.

"That-a-girl," Vanessa reassured, patting me on the back. "Look out San Francisco, the bitches are here!" she shouted and pumped her fist in the air. I lifted mine to match hers, and we laughed. "We should go back to that club tonight. Maybe Lane and Cian will be there even though they won't be performing? Which would be even better since they could spend more time with us."

"I can't tonight. I have a meeting first thing Monday morning, and I really need to get my shit together so I can prepare for it."

"Ah, yes. First day jitters. I can completely relate. I have a few of those myself. You're right. I guess we'll just have to wait until next Saturday, then."

"Sounds like a plan. But weren't you hitting it off with that guy, Tanner?"

"Ah, my dear, sweet Magdalena. You should know me by now. Must I teach you the ways of the single woman all over again?"

I laughed. "Possibly."

"Repeat after me. 'Variety is the essence of true happiness.'"

I was beginning to believe her. Kellen must have found true happiness because it was clear to me that monogamy was not in his current repertoire of good relationship practices.

Putting my thoughts of Kellen and our wrecked relationship aside, I spent the entire morning organizing my room. Just as I placed the last picture of my parents on my dresser, the doorbell rang.

"I'll get it!" Vanessa called out from the living room. "Oh, my. Thank you very much," she said to whoever was at the door.

At that pleasant reception, I strolled into the living room to see her standing there holding a vase filled with a dozen long-stemmed roses. There was one red rose surrounded by eleven white ones.

"Wow, those are beautiful. Are they from Tanner?"

She looked at the name on the envelope. "Nope. They're for you," she said, holding them out for me to take.

"For me? Are you sure?"

"I do know how to read, silly. It clearly says, 'Magdalena De le Rosa.'"

"Magdalena? Nobody calls me tha—"

"Except Cian," she interrupted with a grin that rivaled the Cheshire cat's.

I placed the flowers on the table, and Vanessa plucked the card from the plastic holder it had been secured to. "Here. Open it."

I glanced at her, then at the card. I carefully took the envelope from her, opened the sealed flap that had my name on it, and removed the card.

"Well, what does it say?"

I glanced at Vanessa and then back at the card.

"My beautiful Magdalena,

A rose for a rose, if you will pardon the cliché. But there is no other than the delicate petals of a rose that could ever compare to your rare beauty. Like the red rose in this bouquet, surrounded by all the white flowers, your beauty stands out, while all others pale in your presence.

Please be my guest this Friday evening for dinner. I'll send a car for you at seven o'clock.

Yours,
Cian DeMarco"

I swallowed to try and quench the dry spot in the back of my throat. "Did you give him our address?"

"No. I didn't even give it to Tanner. I took a cab home."

"I never gave Cian my last name either. So, how do you suppose he knew where I lived?"

She shrugged. "He is resourceful, that's for sure. You are going, right?" she asked as she cleared the rectangular glass coffee table of all debris, leaving the flowers sitting in the middle of it. They did look beautiful.

"I don't know. I'm worried about Kellen."

"Who cares about Kellen? I thought you broke up with him."

"I haven't *officially* broken up with him, yet. I'm planning to, but what if that woman who answered the phone *was* just a co-worker. She could have been there with friends and they were all waiting for him to get ready for all I know." There had to be a good explanation for that woman answering his phone.

"Mags, when are you going to wake up? He hasn't even called you. I bet Kellen is whispering sweet nothings into the ear of one of those bimbo lobbyists he hangs out with right now. Literally, as we speak, with his hand up her skirt."

I sighed. She was right. He'd done it before. But, up until this morning, I'd been positive he'd changed. I had loved Kellen. *Had.* But I wasn't so sure I still did. And if I did, wouldn't it sting just a little bit more that he was possibly cheating on me? Again! One thing was for sure, I couldn't go out with Cian until I officially broke things off with Kellen. I didn't want it to seem or feel like I was cheating. I hated that Kellen cheated. I didn't want to be like him.

Vanessa and I spent the rest of the morning and part of the afternoon decorating our new apartment with the items we'd collected from college, and then decided we should hit the stores for some cool and new San Francisco décor. Plus, we shopped for some of the essentials like dish soap and other kitchen necessities, bathroom supplies, etc.

We ventured into a small art gallery and stopped in our tracks in front of one of the paintings. It was a beautiful woman lying on a bed of white silk, looking as if she'd just experienced a moment of complete ecstasy, her heavy-lidded eyes alluring with a silverish-orange glow. Her dark curls hung loosely over her shoulders, stopping just above her naked breasts. She wore nothing but a necklace with a ruby pendant. She lay on her side, her curves sensual and full. Her lower arm was bent at the crook of her elbow, and she rested her head on her hand. The other arm was up behind her, clutching the neck of an equally gorgeous, naked man who lay with her. His dark hair curled slightly over his ears, and his strong, angled jawline was dusted slightly with stubble. It stirred me. The slight appearance of fangs protruding from his upper lip excited me, as well as the small spot of blood lingering at the corner of his mouth. His eyes held more of an orangish sheen than hers—like fire. The couple was beyond sexy. Hypnotically striking.

We bought the picture.

We hung it above the fireplace and stood side by side, facing it. Mesmerized by its beauty.

The picture's exquisite presence bestowed a captivatingly sexy allure to our new home and made the entire apartment manifest the promise of great adventure.

"Vampires are real you know," Vanessa spoke in such a hushed voice I almost didn't catch her words.

"Why do you say that?" I asked without taking my eyes from the beautiful piece of art.

"I feel it. In here." Out of the corner of my eye, I noticed she'd placed her palm over her left breast. A couple of seconds later, she placed her other hand in mine. It was something we did when we recognized the depth of each other's mental imagery; when we realized it was something profound and unusual and felt the need for support.

"If they are real, they must have a very good resource for survival," I said and shivered a bit at the thought of one of them sucking on my neck. "I wonder if all the legends are true and if they actually kill, or just take what they need to survive."

"I think this picture says it all."

"Lust and nourishment without the kill," I agreed.

"Does it frighten you?"

Not sure whether she meant the picture or the idea of vampires being real, I answered referring to both. "No."

Chapter Seven

Cian

"Cian, get your head out of the clouds, man. We are trying to get this song right, and you're just sitting there staring out the fucking window. At what? Darkness? Stars? Come on, man, get in the groove." Lane's annoyance at me was beginning to gnaw at my nerves. I placed my guitar on the floor, leaning it against the wall, and walked out of the room and to the bar. I needed a drink. I pulled down the bottle of scotch and poured two fingers into a tumbler. Didn't even bother with ice. The burn flowed down my throat but quickly turned to nectar as the age-old liquid coated and soothed my anxiety.

I was pathetic. I couldn't think of anything but Magdalena. Why did she have such a profound effect on me? She hadn't returned to the club the entire week. I hadn't seen or heard anything from her. Not even after the flowers and invitation I'd sent. But what did I expect? I hadn't left a number for her to call, simply because I didn't want her to decline. I'd figured if I didn't give a number, she might just show up since she wouldn't be able to contact me to refuse. But now, I feared I might have screwed it up by not giving her a contact number. Suppose she couldn't make it. Not because she wouldn't want to, but what if she fell ill and couldn't notify me. I would want to know if she were sick. I'd need to be by her side if she were unwell. *Gods, listen to your sorry self, Cian.* Maybe the card I'd sent had been too corny. Maybe I should have asked her out to dinner and a movie instead of just dinner. Maybe I should have said I would be there to pick her up at eight o'clock instead of sending a car at seven.

"Cian!" My brother's damn annoyance pestered me again.

"What is it, Lane?"

"You can't just walk out on us. We need you. You're the fucking lead vocal on this song."

"I don't feel like singing right now."

"Do you need blood?" he asked, and I felt his presence close behind me. I took another swig of the scotch.

"No. I'm fine."

"When's the last time you fed?"

"What are you, my keeper?"

He sighed, placing his hand on my shoulder. "I can have someone brought in."

"I told you, I'm fine. I don't need to feed." I honestly didn't care if I ever sucked in another ounce of blood again, unless it was Magdalena's. I hadn't even tasted her, but I knew from her scent it would be the only blood I'd ever have, her essence beckoned and excited me.

"Then for the love of the dead, please come back and let's finish this fucking song."

"Fine." I gulped the last of the scotch down, wishing it would give me the buzz I craved.

Somehow, I managed to concentrate and we finally got the song to the point where everyone was happy with it. Music for me was a necessity. I suppose the same applied to my brother. We'd always performed. Even before we'd been turned. We'd been musicians in London and had been traveling to the States to pursue a new life—a daring young man's dream and an adventure to see if we could make a living. We didn't need the money these days. Being vampires made earning money easy.

My brother and I had traveled to California after having lived for ten or so years in several different states along the east coast. We'd eventually made our way west, settling in various states along the way for several years at a time before moving on. It was difficult to stay in one place longer than ten or so years before people began to make comments about our young appearance, but with the turnover of residents in San Francisco and the ability to compel humans, we hadn't had much of a problem with that. We own Club Royal so there's never any question about our ages, and if there ever is, well, compulsion works very well.

I stood at the top of the Golden Gate Bridge. The city was beautiful this time of the morning, a couple of hours before sunrise. I'd been resolute in my control to not stalk Magdalena. However, my self-control was slipping, and I knew it was only a matter of time before I would lose the battle. Standing here at the top of the bridge with her bedroom window in my sights wasn't helping.

I ached to see her, to touch her, to inhale her sweet, delicious scent. Tomorrow night couldn't come soon enough.

My foot slipped and I began to fall, flashing into space, and soon I found myself on the ledge of Magdalena's building. Damnit. Five short steps and I'd officially lower myself to creepy stalker status. I'd never stalked a woman. I know of several vampires who do, however. Lane is not one, thankfully. At least not that I knew of, and I'm sure he would have told me. I've never had the desire to just sit and stare at a woman before. Not until Magdalena entered Club Royal last Saturday night. Her scent had been strong, and it had pulled me closer.

The next thing I knew, I was standing outside her window, watching her sleep. I'd heard rumors of vampires meeting their soulmates. Someone whose scent drove them insane, so crazy that they couldn't stay away from them no matter how hard they tried. Causing them to do things they wouldn't normally do. In all my two hundred years, I'd never believed the stories. But now. I wasn't so sure. Because whatever it was that lured me to her window—to *her*—was so strong I was powerless to fight it. I wondered if she felt the same.

She stirred slightly and I panicked, not sure if I should dematerialize or just stay still. I opted for the latter, mostly because I was frozen in fear that she would discover what a sick pervert I was. I hoped if I simply stayed still, she wouldn't wake.

I was an intemperate imbecile to think I could stay away. I watched as she sighed heavily in her sleep. I wanted to stroke my fingers through the beautiful dark curls splaying across her pillow and brush the stray strands away from her bosom so I could feast upon her silky flesh. She was magnificent. There wasn't another creature in the entire world so beautiful. It stole my breath to be so close to her.

I glanced around her room, wanting to take in as much of her surroundings as I could, to learn her likes and habits. The roses I'd sent sat on a desk next to a closed laptop. I knew there were many things I could learn about her from that laptop. That would be too much of a violation, though. Vampire or not, I did possess a few moral principles.

Magdalena.

She stirred again as the sound of her name manifested in my mind. She smiled, and I wished I could go to her. Could she be dreaming of me? My cock hardened at the thought.

I needed to be cautious. If she found me standing on the ledge, watching her, she'd hate me and never agree to have dinner with me. Hell, dinner was the least of the things I wanted to do with Magdalena, but I didn't want to reveal my vampirism to her. At least not yet.

One more night until Friday, my love.

Chapter Eight

Magdalena

A cool breeze flowed across my face and I jolted awake. I sat up, startled.

"Who's there?"

No one answered, and I didn't see anyone. But I'd felt a presence, as if...as if someone had been in my room. But that was ridiculous. I was positive that I had locked the window, and it was clear that no one was in my room. But still, a chill ran down my arms and I got up and grabbed my robe before walking to the window to double check. I stood and stared out, fascinated by the view. The lights on the bridge were all lit up, making it all look very majestic, and the entire city glowed with a radiance that made the Christmas tree at Radio City Music Hall seem dull.

I picked up my phone from my nightstand to check the time. It was five o'clock in the morning. Another hour and the sun would be up, stealing away the magical ambience the lights on the bridge and the city rendered.

My throat became dry and I walked to the kitchen for a glass of water. I had a half thought that maybe Vanessa had been in my room, but when I peeked into hers, she lay asleep.

"Silly thought," I whispered to myself.

I gulped down a glass of water then took myself back to my room, stopping at my desk to smell the beautiful roses Cian had sent. They were so gorgeous, and so unusual to have all white roses and one red one, but he'd wanted to make a point I supposed. I picked up the card and read it again. I couldn't stop smiling as I got back into bed. No one had ever sent me flowers before. Kellen had given me flowers on Valentine's Day, but he'd never had any sent to me. I hadn't fully decided to accept Cian's invitation for tomorrow night yet. However, the flowers were very enticing, and the temptation to join him for dinner was growing the more I looked at them.

It was useless to try and go back to sleep; I needed to be up in an hour anyway. This first week at work had been a challenge, but one I felt completely comfortable with as I learned the ropes. Tagging along with Josh, a fellow reporter, had been a great introduction to the news industry. He was easy to get along with, and really knew what he was doing. We'd become friends rather quickly. I loved my job, and the thought that Kellen might not want me to stay in the city made me a bit angry. To think that up until last weekend, I might have actually succumbed to his wishes and quit, moving back to Sacramento with him if he'd asked me to.

Kellen.

I still needed to officially break up with him. I hadn't tried to call him after last Saturday morning when that woman had answered his phone. But he hadn't tried to call me either. Perhaps she'd never told him his phone rang. But still, he hadn't called me to even see how I was getting along in the city. He didn't seem to care whether or not I missed him, and he obviously didn't miss me or he would have called. Another reason I didn't need to continue that loveless relationship. It was clear to me that Kellen didn't give a damn about me.

Almost as if he knew I'd been thinking about him, my phone

sang out the special song I'd programmed just for Kellen's calls. That was going to change.

I almost didn't answer but decided it was best to get it over with.

"Hi, Kellen."

"Mags. Hey, listen, I'm sorry I haven't called you, I've been tied up."

"I bet." I'm sure my sarcastic remark went right over his head since he had no idea I knew he'd been cheating on me.

"I'm coming to San Francisco this weekend. I'll be there Saturday afternoon. I have a business luncheon at noon, but I'm free after that, and I figured I might as well take advantage of the drive to the city to see you, too. We can go out if you want, unless you'd rather just stay home and rent a movie. And boy, I'll tell you, after the week I've been having, relaxing with you by my side is just what I need."

Really? He was coming to San Francisco for a business lunch. A business lunch! Not just to see me. And as an *afterthought*, he decided it would be good to see me. That was the last straw. I couldn't do it any longer. The future I'd thought to have with Kellen was no more than a pipe dream. I needed to stop this right here and now, or I'd find myself a poor little housewife stuck at home with the kiddies while my husband went on business trip after business trip, fucking every female legislator and lobbyist that crossed his path.

"Kellen," I sighed.

"I'm excited to see you, Mags."

"Kellen," I repeated, wondering if I sounded as exhausted as I felt. The Kellen situation had me drained with fatigue. It and the temptation to see Cian were the only things I had been able to think about this entire week. "Don't come here."

"What? Why not?"

"Because I don't want you to come here. I don't think we

should see each other anymore."

"Maggie? What the hell are you talking about? You're my fucking girlfriend."

"That's the problem, Kellen. I was your girlfriend. I was *your* "fucking" girlfriend, right up until you decided to sleep with all those other women. I'm tired of being your doormat. I'm done."

"Mags, come on, baby. You know those other women don't mean anything to me. It's for my career. I have to be amicable. You know it's you I love."

Did he really just admit to sleeping his way to the top?

"It's not just the other women, Kellen. You're coming to the city for a business meeting and are only coming to see me because it's convenient. You haven't called me once this entire week. I just don't think you care about me and I don't think we should see each other anymore."

"What are you saying, Mags? I have missed you! I told you why I haven't called. I love you."

"I don't love *you*, Kellen."

How could I have been so stupid? I could never love a man who would sleep his way up the corporate ladder. Where was the respect in that?

"We're through. Don't call me anymore. I don't want to see you. Goodbye," I said and ended the call.

"Bravo!" Vanessa stood in my doorway, clapping her hands together. "You actually broke up with the cad."

I nodded. "How did I put up with that for so long? I'm such an idiot."

"Nah, you're just too forgiving. But, yay! We need to celebrate. After work today. Let's meet at that little bar on Grant Avenue that we talked about checking out."

"Sure...but just for one drink. I need to come home and get ready for my date with Cian."

"So, you decided to go out with him, after all."

"Yes. Just now, actually." I grinned, looking forward to seeing Cian again. "And, at least now I can go with a clear conscience and not have the guilt of cheating on Kellen hanging over me."

"Mags, I'm proud of you."

It was official. Kellen and I were no longer together. It felt extremely good to be free from him.

"How do I look?"

"Gorgeous. I bet Cian's going to have that dress off in less than two minutes, though.

I gave her an I-doubt-that look, but I considered whether or not I would give in to Cian. He'd been so hard to resist last week, and now that I didn't have guilty feelings about cheating on Kellen, I most definitely wondered. I'd need to be strong, that's all. After all, what kind of girl would he think I was if I gave in to him so easily and slept with him on the first date? I finished the final touches of my makeup and put in my small heart stud earrings.

"Miss Magdalena De la Rosa." Vanessa said my full name in a deep, formal voice, and I laughed. But my eyes widened when they followed her pointing finger out the window and down to the street where a large black limo sat at the curb. "I think your ride is here."

"He sent a limo?"

"What did you expect? He said he'd send a car."

"Yeah, but a freaking limo?"

Chapter Nine

Ciap

A ri was on his way to pick up Magdalena. I chastised myself one more time about not going along for the ride to retrieve her. I should have just driven to pick her up myself. But seven o'clock was still light out this time of year, just before the twilight hour, and I couldn't go out just yet. Too much direct sunlight would drain me of too much energy. Energy I hoped I'd need later in the evening, if you get my meaning. However, draining my energy would be an understatement. Aside from bright sunlight destroying our eyes—a good pair of Ray-Bans were a vampire's best friend since our pupils remained forever dilated—it would also render me paralyzed. To a vampire, the sun was like Superman's Kryptonite. Maybe I should have said eight o'clock. That way I'd have been able to go along. But it was what it was.

The titanium shades on the windows would be rising just around the time that Magdalena arrived, shortly after the sun completed its descent below the horizon. I stood in front of what I now considered the bane of my existence and waited for the goddamn metallic barrier to rise, glancing at the time on my phone. 7:10 p.m. She'd be here soon.

"What's all this?" Lane asked, gesturing toward the small

table set for two by the large picture window as he entered the spacious living room of our house.

"I've invited Magdalena here for dinner."

He picked up the single red rose from its slim crystal vase and held it to his nose. "Nice. But there are only two settings here. What about the rest of us?"

I laughed at his humorous attempt to ease my nerves. He knew I was anxious. I'd talked of nothing but Magdalena all week.

"Right." He smiled and put the rose back in the vase and came to stand beside me. We both stood, staring at the blinds. Waiting for them to open was an event we always looked forward to since we both knew the agony of being held prisoner in a world of darkness. The excitement of counting down the minutes to freedom and the outside world was something we'd always done together. Not that our home was anything resembling a prison. On the contrary, it was a mansion, sitting on the edge of the cliff, in a little town called Sea Cliff, one of San Francisco's most affluent communities. With views of the city, the bay, as well as the Golden Gate Bridge, the luxurious neighborhood we lived in was also the home of a few famous musicians and movie stars.

Lane and I had purchased the mansion in the year nineteen hundred and sixty. Though these days, the county of San Francisco believes it was our great-grandfather who secured the estate before he died; willing it and an extremely large sum of money—that had been well invested over the years—to both Lane and myself.

Fame wasn't something Lane or the others in our band had any desire for. Being vampires, we didn't need the added attention. Fame required daylight appearances as well as questions regarding our ageless appearance. We'd turned down plenty of recording contracts over the years. We enjoyed playing in the club. It allowed us to be ourselves and play what we liked. We still lived and acted like goddamn rock stars, even without the fame.

"Is she on her way?"

Tempted by a Vampire

"Yes."

He nodded. "I'll be sure to make myself scarce the minute the shades go up."

"That would be appreciated. Feel free to stay away all night."

"How about I just stick to the lower levels. I'd hate to think that a human female could become the thorn that separates us, brother. I do have a life, too, such as it is."

I shrugged, smiling. No, there would never be a woman or anything else that could ever come between my brother and me. He was my one true constant in this hell we'd been forced into. "Suit yourself. Just don't interrupt us unless the house is on fire."

Lane laughed. "Noted." He walked over to the bar. "Drink?" he said and pulled down two tumblers, pouring a generous portion of scotch into each without waiting for me to answer. Which I didn't. He brought them both when he came back to stand beside me in front of the fucking closed blinds. "Here."

"Thanks."

"You're nervous."

"I am."

"I don't think I've ever seen you so anxious about having dinner with a woman before."

"Magdalena is…special. I can't put my finger on just why, but I feel it." The rumors of vampires discovering their soulmates came to my mind again just as the shades began to go up, letting in the night, the lights from the bridge glowing ever so beautifully.

I opened the glass doors leading out to the patio. It overlooked the ocean and afforded a miraculous view of both the bridge and the city. Ari, our human friend and confidant, trusted with the knowledge of our curse, had already prepared the area for a night of romance and fine dining.

"You set two tables?"

I shrugged. I'd had Ari set two tables, one inside and the other outside. Unsure what Magdalena would prefer. Yes, I was nervous.

"Too much?"

"Depends. Do you want her to think you're wishy-washy and unable to make a decision?"

"No, I just want her to know I have her best interests in mind."

"That's very touching."

"Boss." Lane and I turned to find Ari standing in the doorway. "The young lady is waiting downstairs in the library. Do you want me to escort her up?"

"No. I'll go down. Thank you, Ari."

"My pleasure."

"Could you have dinner served in half an hour?"

"Will do." Ari turned to leave, his broad shoulders taking up most of the space in the doorway. Ari was a force to be reckoned with and not someone that I myself would ever want to go one-on-one with. Though my vampire strength outshined his human fervor, I was certain that he'd still manage some major damage to my face.

"Wait, Ari." Lane stepped toward the large man. "Would you mind setting up the game room? We'll need four settings at the poker table."

"No problem. I'll get right on it."

"You're going to have a poker game tonight?"

"Don't worry. It's just Gage, Elvis, and Ari. I promise, we'll be quiet as mice and stay downstairs. You'll never know we're in the house. Now, you'd better go fetch your date before she begins to think you've brought her here just to stare at the books in the library."

Taking Lane's cue, I hurried down the steps. My dead heart choking in my chest like it had a vice clamped around it. If I weren't already dead, I'd think I was having a heart attack. I rounded the corner and stood at the door to the library and almost gasped at the beautiful vision that awaited me. Magdalena stood in the library, perusing some of the literary classics Lane and I had collected throughout the years. Most of them signed, first edition hard copies. Aside from our need for blood, Lane and I both had an insatiable hunger for books. Something our mother had instilled in us at a very young age. I stood, admiring her. The black dress she wore looked paper-thin, and the back was completely open down to the top of her very well defined derrière. Another inch and the top of her crack would be showing. My cock stiffened, and I had to close my eyes briefly to contain the lust.

This woman was going to be my undoing.

The idea of a life with a human female wasn't something that I'd ever considered. I'd been with them before, but I'd never wanted to be exclusive with any of them. The sight of Magdalena in my library did crazy things to my soul, if I had one. She was one of a kind.

She pulled one of the tomes down from the shelf, Bram Stoker's Dracula of all books.

"That's my favorite," I said, and she turned with a start, her hand splayed over her beautiful cleavage.

"You startled me," she said.

"I'm sorry." I strolled closer to her. "That is an original. Published in eighteen ninety-seven. If you look at the title page it's signed by Bram Stoker."

She carefully opened the book and turned to the title page. "Wow. This is amazing, Cian. And it's in such good condition. It must be worth a lot of money."

"$15,000.00 to be exact. Last I checked."

She glanced around the library at some of the other titles and tilted her head upward at the full shelves spanning the circular room all the way up to the twenty-foot-high ceiling. "This is all very impressive."

"It's a hobby. Both Lane and I've been collecting for quite

some time. Our mother insisted we learn to read at an early age and I guess it stuck." She handed me the book, and I placed it back in its spot on the shelf.

She smiled. "Um…thanks for sending the car."

"I would have come myself, but I knew I'd be stuck practicing with the band until just a bit ago. I thought it would be best to just send a car." I didn't like lying to her, but it was necessary if I didn't want her screaming and running for the door.

"You have a beautiful home," she said.

"Come." I held out my hand, and she took it. "I'll give you a semi-tour of the house."

"Only semi?"

"Well, I'd never take another man's woman into my bedroom, even just to show it to her."

"I'm not."

"Not what?"

"Another man's woman. Kellen and I…broke up."

"Good to know, but even more reason not to take you to my room. I don't think I'd have the willpower not to rip that sexy dress from your body and glide my tongue over every inch of your skin."

She blushed a thousand shades of beautiful.

I made the tour brief and only showed her the middle level as we made our way toward the living room where I'd had Ari set up the other table. "There are more rooms, but I must admit, I'm beginning to get a bit hungry and thought maybe you are, too."

"Yes, of course." I still had her hand and led her into the room. Her eyes widened with delight, and her smile had me wanting to forget dinner and just rip her clothes off and taste the sweet essence I desperately wanted. "Wow, Cian, this is really beautiful. And this table is lovely," Magdalena said as her fingers skimmed the back of the chair sitting at the small table.

I picked up the rose. "For you."

She smiled and held it up to her nose. "Thank you. Wow," she said as she headed toward the opened doors to the patio and walked out into the night-cool air. "I love the sound of the ocean. We don't live nearly as close."

"Yes, I know."

"By the way...how *do* you know that, Cian? How did you know where I lived?"

"I put you in the taxi. Did you think I wouldn't have the resources to figure it out?" Again, I hated lying, but it wasn't as if I could simply say, "It was easy, I just traced my way along with the cab and followed you home." But, of course, I couldn't say that.

"No. I guess not." She smiled. "I was very surprised to get your note and the flowers. Thank you, by the way. They are beautiful."

"I'm glad you liked them. I wanted you to have something to remember me."

"You're not that easily forgotten, Cian."

I smiled, but I knew I should slow down, not reveal so much of my emotions. I wanted her, but I knew I was wrong for her. *She'll hate me when she finds out what I am.*

"Would you like to eat out here or inside? I had both set up because I wasn't sure if it would be warm enough out here, but we have the fire pit and the heater."

"Out here would be lovely, I think."

I nodded and mentally let Ari know we'd be eating outside, but a soft breeze flowed over Magdalena and the scent of her blood made my cock harden. I pulled her against me and trailed my finger along the side of her cheek and down her neck where her vein pulsed. Her breath hitched when I palmed her breast and backed her up against the wall. I couldn't help myself; I covered her sweet, heart-shaped mouth with mine. My cock was so tight in my pants; I pressed it against her snugly, wanting her to know how much I desired her. She returned everything I offered, which only made me want more.

"Ahem," Ari's rough, deep voice mingled with the frenzied rush pounding through my ears, and I pulled myself free from Magdalena. I turned around and he was gone, but on the table sat a plate covered with a dozen oysters on the half-shell.

I grinned and looked at her. "Do you like oysters?"

Chapter Ten

Magdalena

S oft classical music played in the background. Nothing like the type of music I heard Cian and his band play the other night. There was definitely more to Cian than the bad boy, rocker persona he portrayed at the club where they performed. He was dressed similarly to the way he'd been the first time I met him at the club—jeans and a t-shirt. Except tonight, he wore a dark purple, long-sleeved button-down shirt—a casual and sexy look on him. Particularly since he'd left several of the top buttons on his shirt open, giving me a glimpse of his tattoos. I itched to run my fingers down them and see where they would lead me.

I ached to be in his arms again. I'd promised myself that I wouldn't give in to him so easily, but it was so very difficult. When we'd kissed earlier, and he had me pinned to the wall, I'd thought for sure I would find myself completely naked and in his bed before we'd even had anything to eat. I was half relieved—but left wanting—when someone had cleared their throat, indicating that the oysters were there.

So, we dined on oysters and champagne, listening to soft classical music and the surf pounding against the rocks below.

"Do you like red wine, Magdalena?"

"Yes. Very much."

"Ari," Cian said to a man as he entered, carrying two dishes of something that smelled delicious. He was the same man who had driven me here, as well as the one who'd ushered Vanessa and me into the club last week. "Do we have another bottle of that 1865 Chateau Lafite?"

"Two bottles."

"Bring one, please."

"Sure, boss."

Ari set one of the plates in front me and the other in front of Cian.

"I hope you like lobster. This is lobster risotto, seasoned with leeks and other herbs," Cian said. I picked up a small forkful, being careful not to drop any of the small risotto onto my lap and tasted. It was heavenly.

About five minutes later, Ari came back with the wine and two glasses. He opened the bottle and poured a thimble-sized amount into Cian's glass as if he were a waiter in a highfalutin restaurant, not the muscle-bound, bodyguard/limo driver I knew him to be. Cian sipped then nodded, and Ari poured some into my glass before pouring more into Cian's.

"That's it, Ari. Thanks. Good luck in the poker game."

Cian lifted his glass and waited for me to lift mine. "To you, Magdalena. You are a rare beauty, just like your name."

I couldn't eat much since I was extremely nervous for some reason. I'd never met anyone like Cian. He was the perfect gentleman throughout the meal, always making sure I was comfortable. Cian poured more wine into his glass and topped off mine. Then he picked up his glass and sipped, staring at me. It made me extremely uncomfortable and I stopped eating. "Is something wrong?" I asked.

He shook his head. "Not a thing." Then he reached out and took my hand in his, turning it over, revealing my palm. He held my hand, gently tracing his finger over the top line.

"You have a very warm heart, Magdalena."

"You're reading my palm?"

"This is known, not only from looking at your palm but also in here." He placed his other hand over my left breast, and I couldn't breathe. He left it there for a few seconds as he gazed into my eyes and then removed it, focusing his attention back to my palm. "You have had many periods of sadness and sorrow in love. I am sorry for that."

I gave him a timid smile, thinking of my parents, not to mention that I'd just broken up with Kellen and he knew it. "I don't believe in fortune telling."

"You don't?"

"No."

He ignored my negativity on the subject and continued to softly skim the lines on my hand. I thought of the psychic reader, Tessa, who Vanessa and I had gone to see right before going to the club. She'd said I'd fall…"Oh, crap," I said out loud.

"Is everything okay?" Cian asked.

"Yes. Everything is fine." I didn't want to tell Cian what Tessa had told me about falling under temptation, because I had a sneaky suspicion that he was the temptation I was about to fall into. I couldn't help thinking about the "meeting someone dark" part of that reading, though. Cian was not dark. In fact, his skin was very fair.

He continued to trace his finger very delicately down the center line of my palm, all the way to my wrist and slowly back up the middle, stopping at the point where my pulse beat. He drew tiny circles around my vein, sending shivers up my spine. I felt my heart thump in my chest, and he looked up at me and smiled.

"You're nervous," he said.

I bit my bottom lip. God, yes, I was. But I didn't say anything, only watched his finger circle around as my stomach fluttered with desire for him.

I couldn't take the titillating sensation of his finger any longer. "Could you excuse me, please? I need to use your facilities."

"Of course."

I stood, and he stood as well, pointing me in the direction of the bathroom. I stood at the sink and washed my hands, and when I glanced up to check my face in the mirror, all I saw was an abstract portrait of a naked woman lying on some sort of sofa, her hand resting down by her core as if she'd been touching herself there. I glanced around the small room for a mirror, but there was none. I thought that rather strange, but quickly dried my hands and went back out to join Cian.

When I came back out onto the deck, Cian was standing by the clear plastic railing, staring out at the bridge. I came to stand next to him, and before I could utter a word, his mouth was on mine. My hands darted to his chest, exploring every inch of what was under his shirt. I'd been aching to touch him all night. All week for that matter. He slowly backed me up until my legs hit a cushioned lounge chair and laid me down, his one knee positioned between my thighs. His hand skated up my leg. We kissed, the heat soaring through my veins explosively. I undid the rest of the buttons of his shirt and he shrugged it off. His biceps and pecs were firm to my touch, chiseled to perfection and covered with the most fascinating tattoos I'd ever seen. A small, silver bar was pierced through each of his nipples, and I grew wet as I gently sucked on one of them. His expert fingers found their way to my core and he growled a little, I think, when he fingered the barely-there, slim triangle of panty I wore. I gasped when I heard the quick rip, and watched what was once my red lace thong hit the ground.

"Sorry, I'll buy you another," he huffed into my ear before he shimmied my dress up to my waist, exposing my core to the cool, gentle evening breeze. I almost orgasmed at the sensation of the wind tickling, exciting me. The thought of being outside, completely exposed with Cian exploring my body in the moonlight was slightly overwhelming. So much for wanting to take it slowly. I was helpless in his arms. His tongue laved up the center of my vulva and he continued to lick. His finger found my clitoris and rubbed circles around it. I bucked my hips in response, and he sucked the little nub between his lips. His hands roamed over my thighs and up my backside. All I could do was stare at his dark hair as he made me hot. I trembled.

"Magdalena, you taste divine." He gently rubbed his teeth over my clit before sucking it in again, sending me over the edge.

I moaned his name. "Cian."

He glanced up at me, his deep blue eyes glowing with an intense silver rim. More silver than I'd noticed before.

I hadn't wanted to go this far; I'd wanted to play it cool, make his desire build a bit more, but I had no willpower, the temptation so overwhelming. I wanted him more than I'd wanted any man before.

Chapter Eleven

Cian

L ooking at Magdalena, I felt the pressure build in my testes as
my swollen cock burned inside my pants, begging for release.
I unzipped my trousers, shoving them down to free my shaft.
I'd licked and laved her until I knew she was satiated and her
creamy texture coated my taste buds. I wanted to taste her blood so
badly, my fangs accidentally elongated, and I nicked a spot just
beside her clitoris. With her blood on the tip of my tongue, I
sucked a little, just to get a sample. It was the sweetest nectar I'd
ever tasted. I sealed the small puncture with my saliva. I would not
drink her blood without her permission. She moaned a little, but I
didn't think she realized what I'd done.

Just that small taste of her blood had me extremely excited,
and I couldn't hold back any longer as my desire for her became
stronger than my need for air. The next second, I was inside of her,
never giving her the option to deny me. Though, I didn't get the
impression that she would have as she raised her hips to meet me,
gyrating, pulling me in tighter and tighter, taking me in as far as I
could go. We were starving for each other.

"My gods, Magdalena, you are beautiful," I said, covering her
lips with mine. I kissed her until I was about to climax, and my lips

ventured to the vein in her neck, lingering and kissing there as long I could, then sucking at her unbroken skin as I emptied myself into her.

We lay outside under the stars, her dress up around her waist, her breasts protruding over the top's bodice. I'd never seen a more beautiful picture. She rested on her back, I on my side, gently fondling her breasts. She sighed into the night sky, before turning on her side to face me.

"Cian...I..."

"Shhhh. I know. I'm sorry. I took advantage."

She smiled against my chest. "No, I just wanted to let you know that...well, I should have mentioned this before, but I am on the pill, so you don't have anything to worry about. Plus, I've only been with one man over the past two years, so I'm safe."

"I wasn't worried." I spoke the truth. Vampires couldn't contract STDs, and I was fairly certain we couldn't procreate, though that theory hadn't been confirmed yet. That we knew of, anyway. Lane, Gage, and Elvis were the only other vampires I knew well enough to know that none of us had produced an offspring in our two hundred years of vampirism. Well, Lane and I had been infected for two hundred years, but I had a feeling that Gage and Elvis were older, though it wasn't something we'd ever discussed. We'd encountered other vampires over the years, but there were always so many territorial issues, we steered clear of them. Except for Elvis and Gage, who wanted the same lifestyle that Lane and I did. There were never any territorial or control issues with those guys. Plus, they enjoyed playing in the band and didn't like the killing side of our existence any more than we did. Chelle, Lane's one and only recent mistake, was proving to be a challenge, though.

Magdalena glanced up at me, a questionable frown on her lovely face. "Why wouldn't you be concerned about that?"

"What I meant was, I never thought you were the type of female who gave herself freely to men, so I wasn't worried about contracting anything. And as far as pregnancy, I'm…infertile."

"Oh, I'm sorry."

I turned to face her and kissed the little crease that had formed between her eyes. "Does that bother you, Magdalena? That I can't produce children?"

She shook her head and grew quiet. Of course, it did. "I hope that doesn't change your opinion of me."

"No. Not at all. I'm just surprised. How do you feel about it?"

I almost laughed but managed to keep my composure. To Magdalena, this was a serious question, and I didn't want to say or do anything to make her think that I didn't care about human needs and desires. But vampires really didn't care about those things, and like it or not, I was a vampire.

"I came to terms with it a long time ago," I supplied nonchalantly, hoping that would put the conversation to rest. However, if there was one thing I'd learned over the past two hundred years, it was that the female attitude regarding such matters of the heart—family and love—was never put to rest until they were satisfied that the outcome of said conversation had ended to their liking.

"A long time ago? And how would you know you're infertile? You're young, early twenties, with your entire life ahead of you. And why would you know that anyway? Were you married before?"

Fuck me. I'd just backed myself into a corner on the subject.

"I just know. Let's talk about something more interesting. Better yet, let's *do* something more interesting." I stood and yanked my pants back up, zippering them but leaving the button unfastened. I had plans that didn't require complete dressing. I held my hand out to her. "Come with me."

Chapter Twelve

Magdalena

C ian stood, giving me the complete picture of his beautifully toned, tattooed chest and arms. I took Cian's hand, smoothing my dress down and repositioning my breasts back inside the bodice as I stood. I glanced down at the ripped red lace thong Cian had removed—with very little effort—from me before tossing it carelessly on the ground and giving me the best orgasm I'd ever had. He led me inside and down a short hallway until we reached an atrium with a wide wooden, spiral staircase, complete with a beautiful crystal chandelier hanging from the ceiling. My heels clicked on the Italian marble tile as we made our way across the area to the stairs.

My head was reeling from the mind-blowing sex I'd just experienced, and the knowledge that Cian was infertile, creating two very different emotions in my brain. One pitted against the other for its rightful possession of my immediate mentation. I liked Cian. A lot. And the thought of any serious relationship with him now seemed impossible because family and kids had always been a part of the future I'd envisioned for myself.

At the top of the stairs, we headed down a long hallway lined with photos. Most very old. I guessed they were relatives of Cian's until we passed one that caught my eye. A picture of Cian and Lane together, arms draped around each other's shoulders, huge grins on both of their faces. The photograph itself had an antique flare to it, making it look as if it had been taken many years ago. Way before digital cameras came into play. They appeared to be standing on some sort of luxury cruise ship; only it too showed signs of age.

"Is this you and Lane?" I couldn't help but ask.

"Yes," he said, leading me into another room with a king-size bed in the center and a huge fireplace directly in front of the bed. A large flat screen hung on the wall next to the fireplace with a cabinet below it. X-box and Play Station controllers lay scattered on the floor in front of two large, reclining chairs. I smiled. I enjoyed video games. In fact, Kellen and I had spent many hours playing The Walking Dead game.

"It looks like you play a lot of video games," I said, wondering which games Cian enjoyed.

"Sometimes, when I'm bored. Welcome to my room. There is a bathroom in there if you need it. I'll be back in a few minutes. I'm going to get some drinks."

I decided to take advantage of the alone time and freshen up a bit. I entered the bathroom and stood in front of the sink. Again, I looked up at the mirror to check my makeup and stared into another abstract portrait of a woman in a similar position as the one in the downstairs bathroom. I turned around to see if maybe the mirror was on the opposite wall, but there was nothing there either. No mirrors in the bathrooms at all. "What that hell?" I whispered. "Guys." And shook my head. I freshened up a bit, hoped my hair and makeup were still intact, and went back to the bedroom and sat on the edge of the bed.

I looked around the room; it was enormous. I think someone could live in Cian's room and never need to venture anywhere else in the house, except for wanting to check oneself in the mirror every once in a while, I could become a complete recluse if I lived here. On one side of the room, a circular alcove with a huge picture window protruded out over the ocean below. The cubby housed two plush and comfortable cushioned chairs in a multitude of tan and brown shades with a small table between them. I walked to it to see what sort of view he had, and, of course, I wasn't disappointed. To my right, the Golden Gate Bridge glowed in all its spectacular glory, lit up to perfection. To my left, the Pacific Ocean, as well as another alcove with a window identical in shape to the one I stood inside. I supposed that was Lane's room, and I bet that they'd had both alcoves built after they moved in to present each with the best views possible. I had to admit, it was rather ingenious.

"It is a clear night. I'm glad that you came tonight. Clouds have a way of putting a damper on the view. I've brought some champagne."

Cian handed me one of the flutes full of bubbly, and I sipped.

He set his glass down on a table in the corner, and I did the same. Then he turned me to face him, and his lips softly caressed the side of my neck just below my earlobe. He snuck a finger under the tiny strap of my dress and slipped it off my shoulder, repeating the motion on the other side. My dress fell to the floor, leaving me completely naked as his eyes roamed my body. Normally, I would have felt very self-conscious, but the lustful look in Cian's eyes made me feel sexy. Alive. Every pore of my body begged to be caressed and stroked by his beautiful, skillful hands. I was no longer Mags or Maggie. I was most definitely the Magdalena Cian so affectionately referred to me as—powerful and eloquent.

"Magdalena, I want you so much. Will you let me have you?"

"Yes. I want you, too," I confessed, no longer worried about denying the temptation. I wanted him. Again.

He let his pants fall to the floor and stepped out of them. I gasped a bit at the sight of him. I hadn't really seen him naked the first time we had sex since it had been rather rushed and frenzied, but he was beyond huge. The mushroom head of his cock passed well beyond his navel. He gathered me up in his arms and carried me to his bed, placing me down on silky, black satin sheets that I found to be very sexy and alluring.

I couldn't look away from him. His gorgeous dark hair curled over his forehead and his ears, and his eyes glowed silver around the edges, tugging at the urges in my mind. His taut, muscular chest begged for me to rake my fingers down it. He pulled me up and kissed me. His tongue speared into my mouth, and I wrapped my arms around his broad shoulders. There was no doubt in my mind that Cian, despite his young age, had mastered the art of kissing and lovemaking many years ago.

I fell back on the bed as he came with me, gently, his fingers kneading my breasts, his tongue swirling around inside my mouth before moving on to kiss the length of my throat.

He parted my thighs.

"Oh, Magdalena, so wet for me. You tempt me beyond control."

He had no idea about temptation and control. I'd lost both those battles an hour ago down on the patio. Now all I could think about was how hot he was and how much I needed his hard body against me. In me.

Heat filled my veins and traveled to every cell in my body when he skimmed his hands between my thighs and thrust two fingers inside of me. My hips involuntarily bucked when he crooked his middle finger, wiggling it against my G-spot. His thumb twirled little circles around my clit as liquid heat poured from me onto his hand.

Cian twisted our bodies around so that I was on top of him. We sat facing each other; my legs straddling his hips as the tip of his huge cock brushed against my sex. My heart beat erratically, and blood pulsed at my core. I ached to have him back inside of me. He pulled me against him, close, and he entered. His hips thrust up, hard, and I took him in, felt the tip plunge against my cervix. I'd never been this aroused before, and I came almost immediately.

His tongue circled the spot right below my earlobe, and I felt a heated sensation fill me as he sucked the side of my neck. I'd never had a hickey before; had always loathed them when I saw them on other women or men. But this time, I didn't care, as Cian continued his thrusts, pulling and kneading my hips while his tongue tickled the outside of my throat where I knew my pulse must be beating wildly. Between his gentle sucks, he kneaded and pinched each of my nipples between his finger and thumb. Then he swore, loudly.

"Holy fuck!"

His body stiffened as I felt him empty himself inside of me.

I closed my eyes and fought to catch my breath. The entire experience left me drained, yet wanting more. I'd never felt anything like that before. I snuggled against Cian. He draped his arm over me, positioning one of his legs under mine with the other stretched out beside me.

Chapter Thirteen

Cian

Morning was approaching, and I carefully untangled my limbs from Magdalena's without waking her. I scribbled a quick note for her, explaining that I needed to work and that Ari would be taking her home, and left her in my room. The shades would be coming down any minute, and though I could have stayed with her, I didn't want to have to lie directly to her face about why I wouldn't be able to take her home. This way, I'd already be gone.

I walked down to the large dining area where Lane, Chelle, and Elvis sat drinking coffee, looking every bit the normal human family that they weren't. One of the servants came in and placed a plate of eggs and bacon in front of each of them. Elvis tipped up his dark shades and licked his lips at the food in front of him. He wore those sunglasses constantly. He said he liked being prepared, just in case he was ever caught out in the sun's damaging rays. Aside from his dark strands, slick hair putty, and his long sideburns, the shades were just another reason we called him Elvis.

"Hey, did you know that your brother is keeping me prisoner?" Chelle asked. I gave her a derogatory glance. Her bright red and blue bangs contrasted with the rest of her short, dark brown crop of hair. She was a new vampire, and her opinion about her new life and how she was treated was of no importance. Lane should have let her die, but he'd felt too responsible. He'd been extremely drunk one night and out on a feeding frenzy. Something we usually never did, especially alone. But, like I said, he'd been drunk. By the time I reached him, he'd already sucked all the blood she had to give. When he realized that her lifeless body lay in his arms, he'd cried. In the two hundred years we'd been vampires, I'd never seen my brother cry. I begged him to let her go. Said that I would never think him cruel or a monster, but he couldn't bear the thought of killing her. So he gave her his blood, turning her. She'd been devoted to him after that, wanting to be with him sexually. He became extremely guilt-ridden and apparently gave in more than once, which was a mistake in my opinion. She needed to learn to be on her own if she was going to survive. Her bloodlust and desire to kill was still very strong and sometimes she needed to be restrained. More in the beginning than now, but the thrill of the kill was still very prevalent during her feedings. Lane should have compelled her, but I knew he wouldn't. Like me, he didn't like to compel females, even female vampires. He'd insisted that if he and I could overcome the need to kill without compulsion, then so could she. Now, here she was. His problem. Not mine.

"Lane will keep you a prisoner, as you call it, as long as you continue to act stupid and do foolish things. Now shut the fuck up."

She sank back in her chair, and Lane smirked.

"Breakfast, sir?" the little manservant named Stan asked, looking at me.

"No. No, thanks. Where's Ari?"

"I'm right here," Ari said, walking into the room carrying his own plate. He sat at the table with the others.

"I'll need you to take Magdalena home when she wakes up."

"Sure, boss."

"Keep the explanation simple. Not too much detail about why I had to leave."

"Where are you going?" Lane asked.

"I can't be here when she wakes up. I don't want to use compulsion on her. It's too early to try to explain things to her."

"You can't be serious," he said then bit off two inches of a piece of bacon. "You can't tell her. Ever. Not unless you wipe the knowledge from her mind afterwards."

"Why not? Ari knows about us."

"That's because you saved my life. I trust you, you trust me," Ari said.

"Maybe she will, too."

"Doubtful. We made a pact," Lane said.

"You can't reveal yourself, Cian. It will ruin everything," Elvis added.

"I don't have time to discuss this right now. I need to get out of here before she comes down."

"Why do you need to leave?" a soft feminine voice questioned as Magdalena's beautiful face peeked around the corner at us.

The five of us stared at her.

Someone cleared their throat.

"Yeah, Cian, why do you have to leave?" my brother asked with great amusement in his tone before shoving the rest of the piece of bacon into his mouth. I hoped he choked on it.

I took Magdalena's arm and led her away from the others. "I'm sorry. I was going to have Ari take you home."

"Why? Where do you need to go?"

Just then, all the shades in the entire house began to lower. We stood, and she watched as they all reached the bottom and then made that reassuring, yet obnoxious locking sound.

"Come with me," I said and took her back up to my room.

"Cian, what's going on?"

"I know you have questions. And I know you have a right to answers, but I…"

"Damn straight I have questions. You spend the entire night making love to me, telling me how much you want me, now you're sneaking out, leaving me for your butler—or whatever the hell he is—to take me home, as if you can't bring yourself to face me."

"It's not like that, Magdalena."

"Then why are you trying to sneak out? Why do you need to leave? And why are all the shades closing and locking when it's morning? And as long as I'm on a roll here, why are there no fucking mirrors in this house?"

I stood in front of her, gawking at her adorable exhibition of a temper tantrum. Her hair was a tangled mess, and mascara was smeared below her eyes, but she was still beautiful.

"There are things you don't understand. Things you couldn't possibly comprehend."

"Are you saying I'm stupid?"

"Of course not. You're just…human."

"What? What's that supposed to mean?"

I knew that if I told her and she freaked out and wanted to expose us, I'd need to compel her. But I had to trust that she wouldn't. I also knew the possibility existed where I'd have to compel her if she didn't accept me for what I was, For Magdalena, I was willing to take that chance, because I did not want to lose her. I blew out a frustrated breath of air. "Do you trust me, Magdalena?"

"I'm not so sure anymore."

I swallowed. I was afraid she'd say that. I needed her trust if I was going to confide in her. "Magdalena, I need you to trust me. You need to understand and believe that I will never hurt you."

"The only way you could hurt me is if you tell me you don't

want to see me anymore, because after last night, yes, that would hurt me."

"You have no idea how that concept could be furthest from my mind. I want to be with you, more than I want anything else." I needed her. Now that I'd been with her, there was no doubt in my mind that I needed her more than I needed the blood that sustained me. "In fact," I continued, "I hate the idea of you leaving this house, but I can't tell you anything without knowing you won't run away."

"I won't run," she said, shaking her head slowly. "Cian, please tell me what's going on. Two hours ago, you held me so tightly I thought I'd lose consciousness from the lack of air. You told me how beautiful I was and how much you wanted me. I gave myself to you completely. So, yes, I trust you. What is all this about?"

"Please, sit down."

"I don't want to sit down."

"Okay." I sucked in a wicked breath of air and spit it out.

"I am…*vampire*."

Chapter Fourteen

Magdalena

I had to consciously close my gaping mouth before I laughed, rolling my eyes at his ridiculous statement.

"Come on, Cian. Be realistic. How can you joke right now?" I accused, but something about the way he'd said it had me second-guessing everything I'd ever believed. "I am vampire." Not I am *a* vampire. It just sounded so real.

"I am telling you the truth." His face showed no signs of jocularity. "I will never lie to you, Magdalena."

"You really can't expect me to believe you."

"I knew you'd have doubts."

Vampires are real, you know, Vanessa's softly whispered statement when we'd purchased the portrait came flooding into my mind like a tsunami.

I shook my head.

Everything began to make sense: the hypnosis in the bar, the lack of mirrors in this house, the shades lowering and locking at dawn, his…his, infertility. My knees became weak and the room spun around me. "I…I don't feel so well…I think I'm going to…"

I opened my eyes to see Cian's silvery blue ones. I was lying on the bed while he dabbed something cold on my forehead. "There you are." He smiled.

Oh good, he smiled.

"It was a joke, then?" I asked.

His smile disappeared. "No. I'm afraid not."

I sat up on my elbows.

"Easy."

"This can't be happening."

"I wish, with all my heart, that it wasn't."

"Cian. How is this possible? Vampires are not real. Are you one of those people who live a lifestyle as if you were a vampire? I've been to some of their sites on the Internet."

"There are people like that?" he asked with too much innocence attached.

"Yes." I shook my head. "Maybe, I don't know. Do you have fangs?"

He nodded.

"Why haven't I seen them? Felt them when we kissed?"

"They only show when I'm about to use them. Otherwise, they remain embedded in my gums."

Duh. Okay, so that was a stupid question. "Let me see them."

"You won't like what you see."

I bit my lower lip. "I won't believe you are a vampire without proof."

"If you insist." He stood and smiled, but it didn't seem like a smile. It was more of a snarl, and his facial features became animalistic, frightening, as two sharp teeth appeared. I jumped backwards, the headboard of the bed stopping me from going any farther. I suddenly wanted to run, but I couldn't.

A few seconds later, his face returned to the gorgeous man I'd made love to the night before.

"Don't be frightened. I will never hurt you. I promise."

"How can I believe you? You're a...a vampire." I couldn't believe I'd made the statement. Saying it made it seem even more real.

"Magdalena, if I were going to hurt you, wouldn't I have done it already?"

"Well, maybe you like toying with your food before you eat it." The minute the words left my lips, and in no more than a blink of an eye, his face was inches from mine.

"I do not "toy" with my food," he growled, and I held my breath, knowing the horror that showed on my face as he got up and took a step back and then another. He ran his hand through his dark curls. "I'm sorry. I didn't mean to frighten you."

I wanted to cry.

I was scared. He was scary. But the way his gaze held mine at that moment, the fear slowly slipped away. Though I didn't want to find out what happened if or when that frightening animal came back.

"I need to leave," I said, trying to get up, but my legs were still weak.

"Please don't leave. Not like this."

I wanted so much to trust him, to believe in him, but I was still having trouble wrapping my head around the fact that he was a vampire. A creature of the night. An animal. A blood-thirsty killer. I studied him as he rubbed his hands over his face in frustration. He looked rather angelic sitting there worrying. He took my hand in his. So gentle. He'd been so tender last night. Not a killer. Not an animal.

"You won't hurt me." It wasn't a question. More a declaration, an order that I'm afraid didn't come off as powerful as I'd hoped, considering my trembling voice.

"I won't ever hurt you. I promise."

I placed my feet on the ground and sat on the edge of the bed, feeling a bit less vulnerable and able to get up faster in case I needed to make a break for it. Though I knew I'd never make it, which brought me to the realization that I might as well stay and listen and find out as much as possible. What did I have to lose? And as Cian pointed out, he hadn't hurt me, and if he was truly a monster, he would have already. I had to believe that the man who made such passionate love to me last night would not hurt me now.

I sucked in a breath. "Is it true that vampires can compel their victims into submission?" I asked, my voice still shaking with fear.

"Yes. Most of the time." He let go of my hand and stood. He took a couple of steps, then turned back to face me and waited for my next question.

"Are you compelling me now?" I asked.

"No."

"Have you compelled me? Last night?" If he said yes, I was going to die. I didn't want to think that all those feeling I'd experienced were fake.

"No. And I won't. Whatever you do with me will always be your own will. I promise."

I bit my lip, thinking. I didn't know what I should do.

"You have more questions."

I nodded.

"Go on, ask them."

"Do your fangs really break through skin as easily as it looks in movies and is described in books?"

He gave me a very dangerous looking grin then bit into his wrist. Blood dripped from two small wounds as he turned his arm toward me. Then he ran his tongue over the two red and bloody spots, and the wounds disappeared as though they had never been there.

"So that's how you are able to live? To drink someone's blood without them knowing?"

"Yes."

"Did you drink my blood?"

"No."

"How do I know you are telling me the truth?"

"You'll just have to trust me on that one. But I promise you, I will never drink your blood."

"Good."

"Not without your permission," he added with a sexy grin. "I did not drink your blood, but I must confess, last night, I did take a little taste."

My hands instinctively went to my neck and I had to overcome the desire to run.

"Not from your neck. I accidentally nicked you while I was pleasuring you, but I slid my tongue over it to seal it. It was not my intention to drink that particular fluid from you last night. I had other things on my mind."

My stomach swirled at the memory of his mouth and the things he'd done to me with his tongue and I shook my head to clear the arousing thoughts.

"Have you ever killed anyone?"

"Yes."

I scooted back from him again. Still not sure what to think.

"It's been two hundred years since I've killed someone. Lane and I were turned at the same time. After going on a killing spree together, it sickened us both, and we vowed never to kill again. I will not harm you, Magdalena. Ever."

He sat back down on the bed and faced me, his long legs dangling over the side. He placed his hand over the top of mine. I pulled back slightly but then allowed him to touch me. "I do care for you, Magdalena. Believe that."

"How did it happen? How did you become vampires?"

"While Lane and I were traveling to the States from London,

we met a woman on the ship."

"The picture of you and Lane that I saw in the hallway. Is that the ship?"

"Yes. It was in the year eighteen twelve, and we were twenty years old."

"You and Lane are twins?"

"Fraternal twins, yes. I am the oldest, though."

I chuckled a little at the oldest remark.

"I guess you could say that we were born *and* died together."

"Died? I don't understand?"

Cian's face became serious, and I listened to him tell me about the woman who'd turned them into vampires.

"Her name was Jewels. We never bothered to exchange last names. She left us to die, or rather, wake up to discover the monsters she'd turned us into."

He told me how he and Lane had killed so many people on that boat just so they could survive. I wanted to cry.

He held out his hand. "Please, let's sit by the table for a while and I'll try to explain more about it over some breakfast. You must be hungry. You barely ate anything last night."

"I doubt I can eat now. Cian, this is too surreal. I'm feeling a little nauseous."

"You do look a bit pale, and it is understandable. Some food in your stomach will help."

A few minutes later, Ari appeared at the door, carrying a tray with coffee and a plate of eggs, bacon, and toast.

After he had placed them on the table, he left without saying a word. I turned to Cian. "How did he know to bring food?"

"I told him with my mind."

"You can read minds?"

"It's a bond we share."

"Is Ari a vampire, too?"

"No. He is human, like you."

"Explain this bond."

"Ari's been with us for about seven years now. Lane and I found him beaten up and left for dead in one of Chinatown's back allies when he was only fifteen. He'd been strung out on heroine, and whoever beat the shit out of him had taken all of his money and his ID. He also had no idea who he was. The poor kid had nowhere to go, so we nursed him back to health and gave him a place to stay. He's been with us ever since."

"So how is he able to know what you are thinking?"

"He only knows what I allow him to know. When we found him near death, we had to give him some of our blood to save his life. Vampire blood has a strong healing element to it, that's why it is difficult to kill a vampire. We heal too quickly. He is able to know what I am thinking when I summon him because he has my blood in his system. This also allows me to always know where he is."

"And Lane?" I asked, not wanting to leave his twin out of the story.

"And Lane," he affirmed.

"Why didn't Ari become a vampire after drinking your blood?"

He smiled. "It's not that simple. I or another vampire would have to drink his blood to the point of almost draining him dry, then he'd have to drink a considerable amount of our blood in order to turn. Turning someone into a vampire is not something we like to do. It's a very difficult life."

"But you live forever."

"Living forever in darkness and most of the time alone…it can be very lonely."

I thought about that for a second, and a stab of sorrow flowed through me. "Yes, I suppose so. Are the others in the band vampires?"

"Yes, both Gage and Elvis are."

"Elvis?"

"His real name is Preston. We used to call him Press, but he looks so much like Elvis Presley did back in the late nineteen-fifties, we started calling him Elvis. It stuck after he did a great impersonation of the King one night. We all met about ninety years ago on our way across country. We'd been running from some territorial types..."

I frowned. "Territorial types?"

"Vampires who feel the need to rule over other vampires because they are older and stronger," he explained. "Gage and Elvis helped us fight against them—they are more mature in their vampirism and therefore more impregnable than Lane and me. After discovering our mutual love of music, we formed the band and have been performing together throughout the years. They live close by and frequently hang out here. Like Ari, they are family."

"What about the girl I saw sitting at the table next to Lane? She is beautiful, though she didn't seem to be enjoying herself."

"That's Chelle. She is very beautiful. But at the moment, she's...more of a remorseful mistake to Lane than anything else."

Chapter Fifteen

Cian

I handed Magdalena a piece of toast, trying to take her mind off Chelle. I didn't want to try and explain her just yet. That subject was better kept for another time.

"Here, take a bite." She opened her mouth, parting those luscious pink lips that I wanted to devour with mine. So much.

After a couple of bites of the toast and some of the eggs, she sipped the coffee. I was relieved to see the color return to her cheeks.

"You're not eating. You ate last night. Don't you normally eat? Food, I mean," she blushed a bit. By the blush, I was sure she'd been referring to the oral pleasure I'd provided her last night, not eating people.

I chuckled and touched her hand. "I do. Though I don't require it the way you do. We usually eat for Ari's sake, and because, sometimes, food tastes very good. Like last night. I'm just not in the mood to eat at the moment."

"Why did you say Chelle was a remorseful mistake to Lane?"

"That's a subject for another time."

"Cian, if you want my trust, you're going to have to answer all my questions."

"I already have your trust, or you wouldn't be sitting here."

"True, but if you want me to continue trusting you, then you should tell me everything. Besides, I'll never be able to get through the next several nights listening to Vanessa badgering me about Lane if I don't have all the facts."

"Magdalena, you can't tell Vanessa or anyone about me or any of the others. Please, you must promise me you won't say a word about this to anyone."

"Okay. I promise. But really, Cian, your secret would be safe with Vanessa. I'd state my life on it. She's hopelessly infatuated with Lane, you know."

"You can't tell her. Please, Magdalena, don't make me force you."

"Force me?"

"I don't want to have to make you heed my commands, Magdalena."

"You said you would never use compulsion on me."

"Yes. However, if you insist on revealing our existence, I would be forced to."

"Yes, but…"

"Don't test me on this. I can be very persuasive, and you would never know it."

She swallowed. "So, all of the stories and legends about vampires are true?"

"Some, like compulsion are true. Where do you think most legends originate from?"

"I always thought from someone's imagination, some writer's creation. Like Anne Rice or Bram Stoker. Your favorite. Remember? That's what you said last night."

"It's difficult to keep an existence such as ours a complete secret. There's always a shred of truth behind all legends. Writers and such help fuel the belief that's it's all fiction, but in reality, the legends and stories of vampires have originated from fact."

"So, you would compel me to not remember that you're a vampire?"

"I wouldn't want to, but I would have to. Unless I can get your complete and sincere promise to not breathe a word of this to anyone."

She grew silent, bit her bottom lip and looked down at our clasped hands.

"Please, Magdalena. Don't test me. I will wipe your mind clear of all of this and you will not remember a thing. I don't ever *want* to compel you, but I would do it to preserve our secret, to ensure our existence."

She sucked in a jagged breath. "Okay. You have my word."

"Good. Do you want to go home now?"

"I suppose I should, but then you can't take me. Right?"

"I can get Ari to drive you. It won't be a problem." I didn't want her to leave. Not yet. Not after everything we'd just discussed. I needed to make sure she trusted me and would not divulge anything about my family or me to her friend. But I did want her to have complete free will.

"Yes, I should go home, then."

"Okay."

"Will you be performing at the club tonight?"

"Yes. Would you like to come and listen?"

She nodded.

"May I pick you up at eight o'clock?"

"All right. Is it okay if Vanessa comes, too?"

"Of course, I wouldn't dream of coming between you and your friend. Not in that way, at least." I chuckled.

"Cian!" She studied my face. "Have you done that before?"

"Done what?"

"A ménage à trois."

"I told you how Lane and I were turned."

"That was with one woman and two men."

I shrugged. "I've been in this world for a long time, Magdalena. I've done a lot of things. So, yes, I have."

"So, are you saying you want to have sex with Vanessa and me?"

"I only want what you want."

Chapter Sixteen

Magdalena

The ride home from Cian's was very unsettling at first. I still had a ton of questions. Though I knew I would keep Cian's secret, I still had doubts as to whether or not I wanted to continue a relationship with him.

He was a vampire!

And that was a frightening thought. What was more frightening, was that I had agreed to see him again. Tonight.

There I was, in a limousine with Ari, and from what I'd gathered, he was basically a human slave to Cian and his brother. I sat in the back, still unsure of everything Cian had told me.

"Ari?"

"Yeah?"

"Do you like living at that house and taking care of Cian and Lane?"

He laughed. "I knew you'd eventually ask me that." He glanced at me through the rearview mirror. "Yeah, I do. You won't find two people more decent than Cian and Lane. Not even human ones. They saved my life, you know."

"Yes, Cian told me."

"I owe them a lot. They took me in and let me stay in that

huge house of theirs for free. Plus, they pay me very well for helping them through the daylight hours, doing things they can't do when the sun is out."

"They pay you?"

"Fuck, yeah. What'd you think? I was some vampire slave?"

"I didn't know what to think," I admitted.

"They pay all their employees."

"They have more employees?"

"Who do you think does all that cooking and keeps the place clean? Not me."

"I hadn't thought about it. Do all the employees know what they are?"

"No. I'm the only one."

"Weren't you frightened when you first learned about their…"

"Vampirism?"

I nodded.

"Maybe. A little. But you have to realize that I woke up in that house in a clean room, on a clean bed with nice linens, and I'd come down from a near death high thanks to them and their blood. To wake up in an environment like that after being shitfaced down in a gutter full of puke and urine, believe me, I didn't ask too many questions about my rescuers."

Ari pulled the car up to the curb in front of my apartment building. He put the car in park and turned around to look at me, placing his arm on the back of the seat. "Listen, Cian's got a heart of gold, and I know he'd never hurt you. Try to remember that."

I gave him a smile. "Thanks."

"And just so you know, I'd do anything for him and Lane."

"Thanks for the ride, Ari." I got out of the car and shut the door. In the elevator, I thought about Vanessa. I couldn't tell her about Cian and Lane. I'd never been much of a liar, so I hoped she wouldn't see through me this time.

It was quiet inside the apartment. "Vanessa?"

When she didn't answer, I yelled out again. Still no response. A huge sigh of relief came out of me that she wasn't home, even though I now worried about where she was. It was eight-thirty in the morning. If Vanessa was gone this early on a Saturday morning, that meant she probably hadn't come home last night.

Which also meant that I didn't have to answer all her questions about where I'd been and what had happened on my date. But I knew I'd eventually be seeing her, and I'd need to be prepared.

I sent her a text.

Me: Where are you?

Vanessa: I went out with Tanner last night. Stayed at his place.

Me: Cian is picking me up at 8 to go to the club. You can join us if you want.

Vanessa: Tanner is taking me. I'll meet you there and I want details on Cian.

Me: You and Tanner? Hmmm...

Vanessa: Turns out, the guy has some major skills. Details later.

Me: Ditto

It was good that she'd decided to give Tanner a chance, especially now that I knew about Lane and Cian. It was bad enough that I was seeing a vampire. It would be too much if both

V and I dated vampires, I think. Of course, I'd leave the vampirism out of any details Vanessa and I shared about our sex lives.

I headed to my room, passing by the picture above the fireplace. I stopped to stare at it for a couple of seconds. *They really are real.* I stripped out of the dress I'd worn last night. I had no underwear on since Cian had ripped off the ones I'd worn, and the dress had its own bra sewn in.

I was exhausted. Not only had Cian and I not slept much because of all the sex we had, but after learning everything about him, my mind was also spent. If I were going to be at all coherent tonight, I'd need to sleep for a little while. Too tired to even put on clothes, I curled up on the bed and pulled the covers up to my chin. I closed my eyes, thinking of Cian and whether or not I was crazy for agreeing to see him again.

I turned over on my side and opened my eyes. I must have fallen asleep because the clock on the table said it was six o'clock. I'd slept all day. I needed to get up. I had some major thinking to do, which called for a long soak in a hot bath.

But I was extremely thirsty. I threw on a bathrobe then headed to the kitchen and grabbed a glass, filling it with cold water from the fridge. I gulped it down, filled the glass again, and carried it back to the bathroom.

I filled the tub and expelled a long sigh as I sank down into the very warm water. I'd added in some lemon-scented bath salts to help smooth out all the kinks manifesting in my muscles. I closed my eyes, wishing I could escape the nightmare that had suddenly become my reality.

Cian was a vampire. I just couldn't bring myself to accept that. Even after he'd shown me his fangs and had bitten into his wrist, drawing blood. Vampires were scary creatures, and I'd be lying if I said I wasn't a little bit afraid of Cian and his family. Yes, he'd told me he'd never hurt me, but what if he lost control? What if his brother lost control? Or one of the others in the band? I shook my head. I wanted to believe I could trust him. He'd shown me nothing but kindness and respect all evening. And the way he'd made love to me...I couldn't deny the pleasure he had given me. No, last night I wasn't afraid, so why was I now that I knew what he was? The knowledge didn't change Cian, but it did change my perception of him. I didn't want to be the type of person who judged people based on their race. Wait. Were vampires even considered a *race*? Vampires were creatures of the night. Creatures. Cian had even called himself a creature. Actually, no. He hadn't used the word, creature. He'd used the term *monster*. Cian wasn't human. It was true, when you consider the definition of the word race, it was a classification of a specific group of humans, so technically, I couldn't even use that term. Ugh, I could sit in this tub and argue with myself all evening and still not know what to do.

He hadn't hurt me.

If anything, he'd given me the best orgasms I'd ever had. Sex with him was the mind-blowing kind that, until last night, I'd only had the pleasure of reading about. He said he'd been a vampire for two hundred years. So, that would make him two hundred and twenty years old. That was a long time. Plenty long enough to learn how to pleasure a woman. And I imagined that Cian had been a quick study, even back then. I closed my eyes and let my fingers roam down to the spot that Cian had so expertly pleasured over and over again last night.

Cian, I wish you could be here with me, I thought as I touched myself.

Chapter Seventeen

Cian

ian, I wish you could be here with me.

I sat up as the sound of Magdalena's voice floated through my mind. The single drop of her blood that I had tasted last night must have been enough to allow me to hear her thoughts and be able to track her. She was in her apartment, though I didn't know what she was doing, except that she was thinking of me. I smiled at the thought.

Ah, you made me feel so wonderful last night. I need you and your magic tongue. I've been trying, to no avail, to mimic your techniques with my fingers, but I can't get that same sensation without you.

She was pleasuring herself.

My cock grew hard, and my loosely fitted lounge pants tented.

I wanted to go to her, pleasure her the way I had last night. I glanced at the window. The shades were still down. Fuck me. I grabbed my hardened shaft and stroked it along with the sounds of Magdalena's moans that echoed through my mind. She was having difficulty reaching a climax. She needed me, but I couldn't send back any encouragement. She'd need to take some of my blood for that. I stroked myself, slow at first, listening to her groans and sighs. When the sounds she made became louder and quicker, I lost control. Before I knew it, I'd come all over my stomach.

That woman was going to be the death of me.

I got out of my bed and grabbed a towel from the bathroom. It was time to get up and prepare for the night anyway. Just as I turned the shower on, Lane presented himself in my doorway.

"What do you want?" I asked, knowing full well what he wanted.

"What did you do about Maggie? Did you tell her what you are?"

"Yes."

"Did you compel her to forget afterwards?"

"No."

"Fuck, Cian. You know that's like pointing a loaded gun at us."

"Humph. Then it will only sting for a few moments, and it'll heal as the bullet works itself out, won't it?"

"Damnit. It's going to cause too many problems for us to fix. What if she talks to someone and we don't find out until it's too late?"

"Honestly, Lane. I don't know what you're getting all worked up about. So what if she talks. Who is going to believe her anyway? If the human world believed that vampires really existed, don't you think they'd be hunting us down? Besides, I trust her. She won't say anything."

"I don't like it."

"I don't care." I shoved him out of the bathroom and shut the door then turned on the water.

"You can't just shut me out, Cian! I have a right to my opinion about the safety of this family!" he shouted through the closed door. "I can take matters into my own hands, you know!"

I opened the door and grabbed Lane around the neck, shoving

him back against the wall.

"If you lay one finger on her, I'll bury you in a metal crate so deep in a hole you'll never be able to dig yourself out. Do you understand?"

I eased up on my grip and let go. He coughed a few times.

"You're choosing her over me, your brother?"

"That's right. I love you, Lane, but don't mess with what's mine. I've fallen for her. I can't help it."

"Are you saying you're in love with her?"

"I don't know. Maybe. I've never been in love before. I don't know how it feels. But if it hurts here, in my chest," I pointed to my heart, "as if someone has lit me on fire from the inside, then yes, maybe I do."

"Could be heartburn." He chuckled. "You couldn't possibly love her. You've known her a week, and you've only been with her one night."

"Years ago, do you remember those rumors we used to hear about vampires meeting their soulmates? Someone who's scent drove them insane, so crazy that they couldn't stay away from them no matter how hard they tried?"

"Those are just stories. Don't you think we would have met a few women to love by now?"

"You're missing the point of the word 'soulmate.' From what I am experiencing, the way I feel, I…it's as if I've been waiting for her my entire life."

"Fuck. Next you'll be spouting off crap like; 'she completes me,' or something equally ridiculous."

"I can't explain it. But maybe that is it," I admitted. "Lane. When and if this ever happens to you, you'll understand. I would never harm something that you love."

He shook his head. "You're certifiable if you think she's going to be able to return that love. We're monsters. Remember?"

I knew full well what we were. I didn't need a reminder from my brother. "We don't have to be monsters, Lane. We don't live like other vampires. We don't kill to survive."

"We do have to drink human blood to survive."

"But we don't kill them. You and I both know that we are different. We've always been different."

"That's just because we didn't have Jewels' influence. Do you think that if she ever returned or found us, that we would be able to deny her? Take a look at Chelle. She does everything that I tell her to do, no questions asked. She follows me around like a duckling trailing its mother."

"It's been two hundred years since Jewels turned us and left us to die. You don't seriously think she'd want anything to do with us now. Besides, she's probably dead. Otherwise, how could she have just disappeared off the boat in the middle of the ocean?"

"What? You think she drowned?" He laughed.

"Well, no. But someone could have decapitated her and thrown her overboard."

"I think we would have heard about something like that happening from the other passengers."

"We were unconscious for days, Lane. There were a lot of things that could have happened that we never bothered to find out. Why are we even having this asinine discussion? I've told Magdalena about us and that's that. She won't reveal our identities."

I left Lane standing in my room and closed the bathroom door again, proceeding to take my shower. Magdalena would never divulge what we were. I was one hundred percent certain.

Chapter Eighteen

Magdalena

It was surreal the way my body ached for Cian's touch. Even though the idea of him being a vampire scared the holy crap out of me, there was something so exciting and daring about the whole thing. I'd always been a risk taker, and so I decided to take my chances and see him again. I had to believe that, if he'd wanted to kill me or have me for dinner, he would have done it already. I was really looking forward to some more of that mind-blowing sex we'd had. After all, he and his band had been performing at that club for a few years now, and no one died yet. And after last night, I had no reason not to trust him.

I'd chosen a black dress with a little pearl trim around the bodice that showed just enough cleavage to entice Cian without being ridiculous.

My body tensed at the knock on the door, even though I was expecting it. I could admit, I was still nervous about being with a vampire.

I opened the door to find Cian. Could he be any more perfect? His hair was combed back except for one tiny curl that hung down slightly over his forehead. He wore a black leather jacket over a white button-down shirt and dark jeans. He looked every bit the rock star, but I was looking forward to what would happen after the performance.

I was very tempted to yank him inside, remove all those clothes, and tie him up to my bed so that I'd have him to myself all night.

"Hi," I finally managed, after drinking in all his yumminess.

"Here, these are for you." He handed me another dozen roses.

"You're going to spoil me, Cian. Thank you, these are lovely. I'll put them in some water." Cian waited just outside the open door to the hallway. "Close the door. You're letting the heat escape into the hall."

"You'll have to invite me in," he said.

"Oh. Of course. I'm sorry. I didn't realize. I mean. I didn't know. Please, come in. I'll just be a minute." Cian waited by the door as I put the flowers in a vase and placed them on the table, an uncontrollable grin plastered on my face. I'd never been treated so wonderfully before.

"Better bring a coat. It's a bit chilly out tonight."

I grabbed my coat, and we headed into the elevator.

Cian opened the back door to the limo. I stepped inside, and he followed in behind me.

"Does Ari do all your driving?"

"Actually, yes. I don't have a driver's license."

"You don't?"

"It requires a birth certificate or passport. And, well, I don't have either of those. Though I could compel the clerk at the DMV to issue me one, I sort of like having Ari drive me around."

"What about Lane, or the others? Does Ari drive them around, too?"

"Sometimes. But they've managed to secure their licenses. I just never saw the need. I've always had someone else do the driving. Except years ago, I did enjoy driving around in some of the first automobile models."

"Things must have been quite different back then," I said, mulling over the idea. I had a difficult time accepting that I'd had sex with someone who was old enough to have driven a car that many years ago. But then Cian kissed me tenderly, but with a great deal of passion, and pressed his hand to the small of my back, gathering me in close against him. All thoughts of age left my brain, leaving me with an exciting anticipation of what the evening had in store.

At the club, I sat at the same table we'd occupied last week. Vanessa and Tanner spent most of the time dancing, and I was left on my own again. But I didn't mind. Cian spent a lot of time smiling at me and giving me his attention while he sang, and I felt very special.

Like last week, neither Cian nor any of the band members came out into the club during their break. It concerned me a bit. I'd need to ask him about that later. But at least Vanessa and Tanner sat with me and didn't go out to dance much the second half.

After the band had played their last song of the night, Cian came up behind me. "Magdalena. Let's get out of here."

I was more than ready to leave. I'd had enough of only wishing to be in Cian's arms.

Ari drove us to Cian's house, and we stood outside on his patio, sipping some red wine and watching the city lights. The bridge was illuminated with a golden glow and lived up to its famous name.

"It's all so beautiful, Cian."

He trailed his finger down my cheek. "Not as beautiful as you."

My cheeks warmed, but I shivered.

"Here, put this on." Cian wrapped my coat around my shoulders and I slipped my arms into the sleeves.

"Why is it that you and the band never come out into the club during the break?" I asked.

He shrugged. "We like sitting backstage, discussing the songs we sang and deciding what we want to perform during the second half. We also share our customary bottle of scotch." He grew silent for a moment, then gently rubbed his finger over my lips. "Sometimes some of the female customers wanting to get close so they can be the one to go home with one of us presents problems, as well. It has a tendency to hold up the second half of the show. I'm sorry. I didn't think. You would have preferred I come out and sit with you?"

"Yes. It would have been nice, but now that you've explained, I understand."

He took my hand and pulled it to his lips, showering little kisses across my knuckles, then turned my hand over and kissed my palm, tickling the center with his tongue.

"I want to show you something. But I don't want to scare you," he said.

"What?"

"Wrap your arms around me and hold on very tight. Don't let go, no matter what."

I did as he asked, and he draped his strong arms around me, holding me close against him. Our bodies jolted, and a second later, we stood together on the ledge of his building. Three stories up from the ground. I started to scream, but his hand covered my mouth.

"Shhhh. Don't scream. You might wake the neighbors." He laughed.

"Cian, this is crazy."

"Are you afraid of heights?"

"No, but I can't believe this is happening."

He smiled. "Hold on."

Next thing I knew, we stood at the top of the north tower of the Golden Gate Bridge, looking back at the beautiful city lights of San Francisco.

"Cian. This is miraculous."

"I come up here frequently to think. To watch the city at night. It's calming and makes me feel human."

"Human? There is nothing human about standing on the north tower at the top of the Golden Gate Bridge."

He smiled, turned me around so that my back was against him, his arms around me, caressing me as I looked out across the bay at all the lights on the hills. "When I watch the lights and listen to the sounds of the city and feel the salty breeze lick my face, my neck, I feel alive in here." He splayed his hand over my heart.

His words struck me as sad. I hadn't given much thought to his feelings about his immortality. He'd mentioned something about the loneliness of eternity, but the magnitude of that concept hadn't settled into my brain until just that very minute. "It's not fair."

"What?" he asked.

"That you have to spend an eternity alone."

"Well, I have my brother."

I smiled. "You know what I mean."

"Yes. I do. Until I met you, I'd resigned myself to the idea of spending eternity alone. But now I can't imagine doing so."

The significance of his last statement hadn't slipped by me unnoticed, and as he kissed me, I suddenly couldn't imagine a life without him in it. Intense heat soared through my body. He slipped his hand under my dress and skimmed up between my legs. The rip of my panties made me laugh. "You're going to have to take stock out at Victoria Secret if you keep that up."

"For you, anything. Magdalena, I need you. The temptation is so difficult to resist."

"I thought I was the one being tempted."

"It's different. I want to make love to you."

"Yes. I want that, too."

"No, you don't understand. I want to make love to you as a vampire."

"How is that different?" I knew what he wanted. I wasn't that naive to believe that he would never want to drink my blood. I'd read the fantasy books about blood drinking and sex and how they always went together, but that's all it had been. Fantasy.

"The allure of your blood has my head spinning. Being up here, at the top of the bridge, I can't think of a better place for your first time."

I swallowed. "My first time?"

"There is no greater sensation in the world, Magdalena."

My stomach knotted and I felt the wetness accumulating in my core as my heart pulsed with desire for him. The idea of him drinking my blood should scare the hell out of me, but temptation, the desire building inside of me, and the need to know how it would feel was winning over.

"I'm scared," I whispered.

"I won't hurt you. I promise. Do you trust me?"

I wanted to trust him. As much as this whole new experience scared me, I wanted to take the chance. "Yes, I trust you." I knew this was right, as much as my heart beat for me, I needed to give some of that to Cian."

"Will you let me?"

"Yes." I closed my eyes, taking in every pleasurable moment of his touch. I heard the sound of a zipper.

"Open your eyes, my love. Watch the city. I love you, Magdalena, with all my heart," Cian whispered right below my ear then he thrust his hard shaft inside of me. When he sank his teeth into my neck, my eyes shot open and I stared into the star-studded sky. It didn't hurt, and I let out a delighted moan, astonished by the pleasurable sensation of his gentle sucking. I tugged him closer, urging him to take from me. A euphoric high soared through my mind as endorphins raced through my veins and my desire to give him everything that I had enveloped me, coating me with a nirvana I never knew existed. I climaxed over and over again as he pumped into me from behind. As he took in my nourishment, I wanted to be everything to this man.

"Cian!" I shouted into the night. My mind flooded with a surge of emotions that I had no control over. The sensation was so overwhelming, the stars in the sky faded away and everything around me went black.

Chapter Nineteen

Cian

Magdalena's blood flowed into me, cradling me. Warming me. The excitement so powerful I was overwhelmed. I'd never tasted anything so heavenly before. It had been a week since I'd drunk from anyone directly. From the minute I'd met her, I vowed to never drink from anyone but her. It had been well worth the wait. This time was different for me.

There was something in her blood that gave me more strength than I'd ever known before. As I sucked at the vein in her neck, I pumped my cock into her. Hard. Both sensations together brought me to a new state of ecstasy. As if heaven itself had reached into the dark depths of hell and grabbed my soul back from within the pit of fire. No drug existed on this planet, strong enough to match the high. She reached behind her and pulled me tighter against her when I began to suck. Her acceptance of me heightened the thrill.

She screamed my name into the night air. I didn't care up here on the bridge. She could scream all she wanted. A million beats of pulsating tingles shot through my veins with each thrilling sound and movement she made. As I emptied every ounce of semen I had into her, she grew quiet, her head resting on my shoulder.

"Magdalena," I whispered into her ear, but she stayed still and silent. I picked her chin up to see that she'd lost consciousness. Had I taken too much? I licked the wounds closed, her slight pulse on the tip of my tongue almost undetectable.

I cradled her in my arms and flashed us both back to my bed where I laid her down. Her beauty brought me to my knees. I knelt beside the bed and rested my head on the edge of the mattress next to her, tears stinging my eyes.

I had taken too much, and now she was weak. I worried that she might not come back to me. I knew there was the possibility of this happening. That I would enjoy her too much and take too much, sending her into a coma. A coma that I could never bring her out of. Fuck, I wanted to break my own fucking neck for going so far.

She stirred. A slight moan. But it was enough. She wasn't in a coma. Thank the gods. She wasn't dying, but she *was* very weak, and she may be sick for a few days.

I let her rest there on my bed, and I stood, zipping up my jeans that I'd left undone while I'd carried Magdalena in my arms back to safety.

I pulled the blanket up over her small, delicate frame and walked to the alcove, staring out at the bridge where I'd sealed Magdalena's fate. She'd never be the same. Oh, she'd still be her, still be the same sweet, wonderful woman I'd locked eyes with sitting inside of that little restaurant before heading to the club. But now, she belonged to me. I'd ensured that tonight when I'd drunk her blood. She would forever flow through my veins.

"Cian," Magdalena called to me. I raced to her side.

"Yes. I'm here."

"What happened?" Her voice music to my ears.

"You scared me. I thought I'd lost you."

She shook her head. "No. It was beautiful, but I'm afraid I must have passed out."

"Because I almost killed you. I'm so very sorry. It was stupid of me."

"Am I a vampire now?" she asked in a sweet, angelic voice. I had to laugh.

"No, my sweet. No. You would have had to ingest my blood and die. You didn't drink my blood, and you certainly did not die. You're just…bonded to me now."

"Oh, is that all," she closed her eyes. "I'm so tired."

"Rest. I'll be right here."

"Magdalena. Wake up. The sun will be up soon. I need to take you home. You have work today."

"I do?"

"Yes. It's Monday, a little after four in the morning."

"Oh. I slept through yesterday?"

"You did. I'm sorry. It's all my fault. I drank too much. I will learn to pace myself next time."

She sighed. "It's okay."

"No, it's not. I will never do that again."

"But I want you to. It…it was amazing."

I smiled. "Yes, it was amazing. I meant I would never take that much from you again. It was the first time, and it had been a while since I'd drunk directly from a human. And I've never taken from anyone who stole my heart before. The taste of your blood consumed me more than I realized. I took too much from you. I promise never to take so much at one time again."

She sat up. Touched my cheek. "I trust you."

"That pleases me. Here, I have something for you." I held up a gold-toned heart pendant dangling from a sturdy gold chain. The pendant was a set of marcasite angel's wings surrounding a large ruby, as if the feathered appendages enfolded a heart of fire. "This belonged to my mother. My brother and I each gave her one right before we left for the States. This one has my name engraved on the back. Mom held both hearts fisted in her hand when she slipped from this world, as if she wanted to carry the memory of us with her. I want you to have this one."

"Oh, Cian, it's beautiful."

"Here, let me put it on you." She pulled her hair free from her neck, and I slipped the chain around her and secured the clasp."

"I'll never take it off," she said.

"It's double clasped for extra security."

"How did she die?"

"It was a long time ago."

"Yes, but...did she know what you and Lane had become?"

"No. We were here in the States. She stayed in London. She was a wonderful woman, always encouraging us to be our best. She taught us how to play the piano and coached us in our singing lessons." I chuckled at the memory. "I miss her, so does Lane. That song I sang and dedicated to you that first night at the club?" She nodded. "We wrote it for her."

"It's a beautiful song. I remember hearing it on the radio. It came out right around the time my own parents died. I listened to it over and over again. It gave me comfort."

"I'm sorry you lost your parents but I'm glad it gave you comfort. And now, like this necklace, the song belongs to you."

The color in her face drained a bit as she stood, teetering on her feet. I held her around her waist to steady her.

Do you feel all right? Maybe you should call in sick from work today."

"No. I can't. I'm still in training."

"Come on, then, let's get you home now, or you'll have to wait until Ari wakes up to take you. Then you'll be late for work."

I teleported us to her apartment, not wanting to bother anyone else to drive us. We materialized inside her bedroom where I knew our sudden appearance would go unnoticed.

I still had a couple of hours before the sun came up, so I

decided to stay just a little while.

We entered the living room and I glanced around. I'd been in her bedroom without her knowledge, but I'd never been in any of the other rooms. Even when I'd picked her up I stayed by the door. The hairs on the back of my neck stood straight up as I turned to see what could be having such an effect on me and stared straight into Jewels' eyes.

"Magdalena, where did you get this picture?"

"Oh. Some little art gallery on Union Street. Isn't it magical?"

I glanced at her. The childlike expression on her face, so full of awe and beauty, rendered me incapable of thinking. But, the possibility of Jewels being alive, here, in San Francisco, frightened the hell out of me. And the thought that my beautiful Magdalena may have had a dangerous encounter with the beast, even more so. "Yes, it is. How long have you had it?"

"About a week. Vanessa and I bought it the day after we moved here. Why?"

I shrugged as if it weren't important. No need to alarm her about something that she probably would never need to know. I needed to talk to Lane, though. If Jewels were in the city, that meant she was feeding. And possibly siring more vampires. The thought of her doing to others what she had done to Lane and me, sickened me. In all of our vampire lives, I had never turned a single human. And we had both gone almost an entire two hundred years without turning anyone until Lane had his unfortunate accident with Chelle. It was barbaric and cruel to sentence an innocent to this life of darkness. Though, the portrait did look as if it had been painted many years ago, artists could give their work any type of texture and background they desired.

"I'm starving." Magdalena's voice brought me back from memories of my sordid past, and I went to her and caressed her cheek with my palm.

"It has been a whole day since you've eaten. Again, I'm sorry."

"Stop saying you're sorry. I wanted it. I let you do it. I could have said something when I started to become weak."

"No, I doubt that."

She sighed. She had no clue what I'd done to her. The power I had over her from the minute I'd sunk my fangs into her vein.

"I'll make some eggs. Do you want to eat?"

"No. I think I'd better get going. I have some things to do before the sun comes up."

"Oh. Are you going to...you know, feed?"

"No. I think I've had enough of your blood to sustain me for a while."

"Cian, you said you don't kill when you feed."

"That's true."

"How do you get them to let you drink their blood?"

"I compel them. They let me feed, and then I wipe their memory of it."

"I guess that's okay. As long as you're not hurting them."

"I promise; it has never been anything more than what I did to you, only without the added bonus of a wonderful orgasm." I grinned, but in truth, I would never drink from another now that I'd had Magdalena.

I closed the short gap between our bodies and kissed her cheek. "Since I've met you, Magdalena, I have not fed from anyone until last night with you. I have no desire to be that intimate with anyone but you ever again."

She sighed into my chest. Lifting her chin with my finger, I kissed her plump lips and darted my tongue into her mouth. She moaned as her tongue scraped under one of my fangs that, like the hard-on in my pants, had a difficult time keeping its presence hidden from her.

Back at the mansion after a short discussion, a very pissed off Lane threw a half full glass tumbler into the fireplace, Sparks hissed and exploded in the air as the very expensive scotch mixed with the flames. "This is un-fucking-believable," he shouted. "Are you sure it's Jewels in the picture?"

"Positive. I could never forget her face. It's haunted me for two hundred years."

"Me, too," he admitted.

"What are we going to do?"

"What can we do? I'm not going to seek her out."

"No. Maybe we should cancel performances for a while. Take a break. A vacation. We could go to Mexico for a bit."

"Live our miserable lives running from a phantom presence? No thanks."

Chapter Twenty

Magdalena

Two weeks had passed, and I was completely and utterly certain that Cian would never hurt me. Each time he and I made love, I allowed him to take my blood, which was every night, sometimes three or four times. He never took as much as he had that first encounter, as his control became stronger and greater each time. He had insisted that I take iron supplements three times a day, and he pumped me full of foods rich in protein like red meats and poultry. After each amazing sexual experience, he brought me a huge glass of orange juice and a chocolate chip cookie. At the rate we were going, I'd need to go on a diet soon.

I didn't know how I'd once considered sex so amazing before, now that I knew how it felt when he drank from my vein during an orgasm. My panties became wet every time I thought about it.

Just as I was certain that Cian would never hurt me, I was sure that his brothers would not either. Lane, of course, but I'd come to call Ari and the other two guys in the band his brothers, as well. It was just easier when talking about them. Cian referred to them as his family, so I did too. I still had so many questions about their lifestyle. I found it fascinating, wanting to know how everything felt to them. Their senses of everything, always much more heightened than mine. I was a little jealous, but as much as I grew to admire and trust Cian more and more each day, I didn't want to be a vampire. I wanted to have kids some day, and I knew that I would never have that with Cian. A sad fact, and one that I struggled with, my heart always winning the battle over the dilemma of ending our relationship. But I feared that I was falling in love with him, which made everything even more difficult, knowing that I would eventually need to end things with him if I wanted to have a normal life.

I picked up my phone from the table where I'd left it last night. A missed call. I checked to see who'd called and frowned when I saw Kellen's name appear. He hadn't left a voicemail. He hadn't shown up that weekend like he'd said he would either; just one more reason I was glad I had broken up with him. He never followed through. But I supposed I should be happy about that. I hoped he wasn't calling to say he was coming this weekend.

It was half past seven when I finished applying my makeup and fixing my hair. I had some time to spare, and before I slipped into the red dress I'd chosen to wear tonight, I decided to pour myself a glass of Chardonnay. I took the wine back into the bedroom with me, and as I sipped the cool liquid, rich with buttery undertones, I studied the red dress that lay on the bed, wondering if Cian would like it. It was my favorite cocktail dress, and one I always felt sexy while wearing. It was perfect for Club Royal.

I pulled the dress over my head. It was a halter-top—another no bra night. As I smoothed the bottom down, glancing in the mirror to make sure I had it all straight, I realized the dress hugged my rear end a little too snugly. "Crap." I must have gained weight since the last time I'd worn it. Those cookies were going to need to stop being a part of my after sex routine.

It was already five minutes to eight, and Cian would be here any minute. I put on my red, strappy, high-heeled sandals and grabbed my purse as the doorbell rang. I smiled. Right on time. He'd get points for that. But I had to imagine that vampires were probably always punctual, considering they could move faster than light. I checked the mirror for any last minute wardrobe faux pas, and couldn't hide the grin on my face at the thought of another—and probably more exciting—night with Cian.

I opened the door to find Kellen standing there.

"Kellen. What are you doing here?"

"I'm here to see you. I told you I was coming."

"That was four weeks ago. And I told you not to. It's over between us."

"You can't mean that. You're just angry. You'll get over it."

"Kellen, I have a date tonight."

"What? A date? Who is he? I'll kill him."

"What are you talking about? You can't kill someone just because I'm dating them."

"Wanna bet? Come on, Mags. I love you. You can't go out with someone else."

"You have a weird sense of what love is, Kellen. Why shouldn't I go out with someone else? You do it all the time. Listen, I don't have time for this." Shoving Kellen back out past the doorjamb, I pulled the door to the apartment closed and locked it behind me. I'd rather take my chances of Kellen and Cian meeting outside in public. I knew Kellen wouldn't be able to hurt Cian, but just the idea of him wanting to, bothered me.

I walked down the stairs, Kellen right on my heels. "Mags, come on. I drove all this way. You can't just leave me hanging. What will I do?"

"I don't care what you do. Just don't be here when I get back."

I walked out of the building just as Cian's limo pulled up to the curb. Cian stepped out of the back.

"Is this the guy?" Kellen said, pointing at Cian.

"Please, Kellen. Go back to Sacramento. I'll call you

tomorrow."

"Hell if I will. Hey, dude," he said, shoving his palm against Cian's shoulder. "This is my girlfriend."

"Pardon?" Cian said in a calm voice then placed his hand on my back before opening the car door for me.

"That's my girlfriend you have your hand on." Then he growled. Kellen actually growled, like a wild animal.

"Get in the car, Magdalena, and don't open the door." I looked at Cian. His face contorted and his fangs dropped. Oh my God! What was happening?

I sat in the back seat of the limo, staring at the unbelievable scene taking place before my eyes. Kellen's limbs vibrated, and huge, sharp claws extended from his fingertips. Razor-sharp teeth snapped as his nose and jaw extended, then his growl filled the night air again. It was dark and difficult to see, but I couldn't take my eyes off of him and Cian as they circled and growled at each other.

I went for the door handle to get out. I had to try and help Cian and talk Kellen's rage down.

"Stay in the car and do as Cian told you," Ari said. I'd forgotten he was in the front seat.

"Ari, what's going on?"

"Well, it looks like your ex is a werewolf."

"A what?" That was impossible.

"Cian. He'll hurt Cian."

"I don't think so."

I sat in the car, watching helplessly as Cian and the thing that used to be Kellen—which was mind-blowing—circled each other several times, snarling and stalking like animals. They *were* animals. Then I heard Kellen snarl out something that sounded like, "This isn't over," and then he took off, disappearing into the night.

Cian opened the car door and got in, his fangs gone, his features completely back to normal.

"Drive," Cian ordered.

"Cian, what just happened?"

"You didn't know your ex-boyfriend was a werewolf?"

"No. How would I know that? How is that even possible?"

"Magdalena. You *are* talking to a vampire."

"Yes, but I've known Kellen for two years. He's never given me any indication that he had that…that…whatever it is he has."

"The ability to shift into a wolf. Though, lucky for us, we were in an alley in the city and he didn't shift completely. I could have held my own if he had, but I doubt I'd be performing tonight after an attack like that."

"You mean if he had turned completely…" I couldn't believe what I was hearing. "You could have been killed?"

"He's a young wolf. Not mature enough to have the strength to kill a vampire. Though, he would have hurt me enough to keep me from singing tonight. But I would have done some serious damage to him, as well. I knew he wouldn't shift all the way, not there in the alley. But that's not the last we've seen of your slimeball ex." He smiled and kissed my forehead.

"He thinks he has a claim on you, and he'll want to fight me with everything he has. Eventually. Werewolves are despicable creatures. It's a genetic affliction."

"You mean his parents were werewolves?"

"Maybe, maybe not. The disease may have lain dormant in his line for generations. It's possible his parents were not aware of it, but one can never be sure without meeting them face-to-face. Not something any vampire would want to do, and it matters little to us. But werewolves and vampires can most definitely sense each other, and the repercussions are rarely pleasant if they share the same space.

"A werewolf cannot control their emotions as well as a

vampire. We are calm and arrogant in their presence. They don't like it, and if we make them angry, well, they have a difficult time controlling their tempers around us. Hell, they have a hard time controlling themselves anytime they get angry. You've apparently never made him angry enough before. But one sniff of my scent sent him into a frenzy."

"So, he sensed you were a vampire."

"Yes, as I immediately recognized what he was. Magdalena, has he ever bitten you?"

"No. Of course, not."

"Not even when...during sex?"

I shook my head. "No."

"Good. Then he hasn't actually claimed you as his."

"I'm no one's property, and I never will be," I huffed and crossed my arms over my chest to make the point.

"If he had bitten you, you might feel differently, which would make my plight more difficult."

"There should be some Vampire/Werewolf 101 course at the community college."

He chuckled. "There's not, but I suppose there should be."

I sighed. "I was joking."

"I know. And I'm glad you can joke about it. I hope that means you're beginning to accept what I am."

I was beginning to, until tonight. I didn't think I'd ever be able to accept what had just happened between Kellen and Cian.

"No. I'm afraid that's going to take a bit more time. I'd say the joking is more a nervous habit that I have during moments of high stress."

Chapter Twenty-One

Ciap

" **A** re you serious?" Lane snapped when I told him and the rest of the band about what had happened with Magdalena's ex. The four of us sat backstage, having a few drinks while we waited to go on. I'd left Magdalena sitting at one of the front tables with Ari and her friends.

"As serious as a plump, throbbing vein," I confirmed. "The guy's a fucking wolf, and I'd bet my right nut that he's going to show up again before the night's through, wanting to stake his claim on Magdalena. I felt him stalking the entire ride over here."

"Fucking wolves have serious territorial issues when it comes to their bitches. No offense," Elvis said to me.

"None taken." I knew he wasn't exactly calling Magdalena a bitch, though if it had been anyone but Elvis or another one of my brothers, I'd have flattened him for the comment.

"They're worse than the fucking vampires who think they can rule others, making stupid rules," Elvis added.

"Has he ever bitten her?" Gage asked.

"No. She had no idea what he was."

"Then from what I know of werewolf ethics—by the way, that's an oxymoron if I ever heard one—he hasn't actually claimed her as his," Gage said.

"Right." I needed to make that clear in my own mind as well as theirs. I needed their help with this. If Kellen did show up in this club, he would most definitely shift completely, and I'd never be able to defend Magdalena on my own. Of course, even if they thought Magdalena had been claimed, they would never just stand by and let a wolf try to take me down.

It was time to go on. We all walked up the six short steps to the stage and took our places.

"Where's Chelle?" I asked Lane as I walked past him to my spot on stage.

"She's secure in her room."

"Good." I knew Lane hated restraining her with fetters, but the last thing we needed was a newbie female vampire fucking things up further if Kellen did show up. It would be bad enough compelling everyone into believing that what they'd seen never happened. Having an uncontrollable new vampire around would only make things worse. One thing at a time. I sighed and pulled the microphone to my mouth.

"San Francisco!" I shouted. "Are you ready to party?"

The crowd roared, and some banged their palms on top of the tables for added effect.

"Are you having a good time?"

More cheering and table banging.

"Let's rock!" I strummed the first chord of the night, a fast song and a favorite, one of the Eagles' greatest hits, to get everyone in the mood. The crowd roared, and the dance floor filled with patrons flailing in wild abandon. There was going to be a bloodbath here tonight. I could smell it in the air. Somebody *was* going to hurt someone before the night was through, and I had a good feeling it was going to be a stupid young wolf. Even though we didn't kill humans for food, that didn't mean we wouldn't enjoy killing a werewolf. We were vampires, and the monster in me smiled, even though the thought of Magdalena possibly getting hurt made me sick.

An hour went by, and there was still no sign of Kellen. Maybe I was wrong. We finished the last song and the room boomed with applause. I sighed as Lane patted me on the back. "Let's take a break," he said.

"San Francisco! You're all rock stars tonight! We're the Lost Boys, and we'll be back right after a short break," I said when the clapping settled down.

I normally stayed out of the club during breaks. We all did. But tonight, we all made our presence known out there. Lane and I pulled up chairs at the table where Magdalena and the others sat. The guy who'd been hanging around the women last week scooted his chair closer to Magdalena's friend when Lane and I sat down.

"Are you all right?" I whispered to Magdalena.

"Yes."

"He's going to be here, you know."

Her beautiful, innocent eyes shot up to mine. "How do you know?"

"I just know," I said and kissed her lightly on the lips, lingering as I gently slid my mouth over hers before sucking in her bottom lip. The taste was heaven. It was useless to try and describe intuitive senses to someone. It wasn't something tangible that one's mind could comprehend unless they'd experienced the feeling.

I pulled back from her the minute the wretched scent entered my nostrils. Lane's eyes fixed on mine. I turned to see Kellen step out of the dark hallway that led into the club from the front door.

"Here we go, boys," Lane grinned. "This ought to be fun." He cracked his knuckles, then his neck. Ari did the same, and I almost laughed. The human was strong, but not strong enough to go against a werewolf.

"Stay back, Ari, take the women upstairs," I ordered, and he immediately grabbed the arms of both Magdalena and Vanessa and quickly ushered them away.

"Maggie!" Kellen yelled over the cacophony of the crowd, and Magdalena stopped then wiggled her way out of Ari's grasp.

"Stay with Ari," I yelled.

"No. I won't let you do this. Not when I know I can prevent it."

I hissed.

"Stupid female," Kellen uttered. "There's nothing you can do to prevent this now, bitch. I just wanted to make sure you knew I was here to kill this bastard. No one takes what's mine."

"I'm not yours," Magdalena yelled.

"Magdalena! Go with Ari! Now!"

She shook her head. "You can't tell me what to do."

Of course, I could. But I didn't want to. Ever.

"As you wish," I said through a fanged jaw, not giving a rat's ass who saw me. I braced for the attack.

Kellen's entire body vibrated and his nose and mouth elongated the same way it had in the alley, but this time, bones crunched and his clothes ripped away as he went down on all fours, his entire body now covered with dark black fur, his jowls salivating with the prospect of a kill.

"What the fuck?" Vanessa yelled. "Kellen's a werewolf?"

He growled and sprang forward. I pivoted too quickly for him and was able to twist my body so that I could sink my fangs deep into the side of his neck before he knew where I'd gone. But he managed to sink his razor-sharp teeth into my shoulder before shrugging me off as though I were an old rag doll. My body hit the wall, and I felt the drywall cave in. Fuck, that was going to require a contractor.

People in the room scattered and screamed. I heard Magdalena call out my name, but I didn't look at her. Didn't want to lose my focus.

The wolf was strong, but not strong enough for four vampires. Lane, Gage, and Elvis bared their fangs and grabbed him, each sinking their teeth into his hind legs. I managed to regain my balance, let the blood coagulate in the wound on my shoulder, then went for another bite. This time, I managed to puncture his jugular. His blood oozed into my mouth and tasted vile. I spit it out, not wanting to swallow it; goddamn, wolves were fucking nasty.

With Gage and Elvis now on each of his front limbs, Lane sank his fangs into the other side of Kellen's neck. The three extra vampires had surprised Kellen. He hadn't been expecting that. You see, once you're in a room with one vampire, it's nearly impossible to sense that there are others close by, unless you know the signs. And as I'd hoped, it was clear that Kellen did not.

We all backed off and let the wolf slump to the floor. We hadn't killed him. But he was injured to the point where he would be limping for a few weeks.

"Magdalena was never yours, you slimeball," I said, taking pleasure in using Vanessa's childish term. "Do you think I'm ignorant of your ways? You never claimed her in the way of the wolf and you never will. Get the fuck out of here before I call the rest of my family in here to finish you off."

Kellen slowly transformed back into a man, then, one leg at a time, he stood.

I picked up his torn clothing and threw the pile of rags at him. "Cover yourself. You look pathetic."

He caught the rags and turned toward the door. He took one last look back at Magdalena, defeat clear in his eyes, then walked out of the club.

Magdalena came running at me, threw her arms around me and buried her face into my chest. "You okay?" I asked, stroking her head.

She looked up at me. I wiped away the wetness on her cheeks with my thumbs. "Yes. Are you?"

"I'm fine."

She looked at my shoulder. "He bit you."

"I'll live." I tugged the neck of my t-shirt down to reveal the now nearly healed wound and she gasped. "We heal quickly."

"I was so scared for you."

"No more scared for me than I was for you, my love."

"I love you, you know."

I nodded. "I know."

"Mags! Move away! Are you crazy? He's, he's...they're all vampires!"

Magdalena turned toward her friend. "Yes, I know. And Kellen is a werewolf."

"But, how? You knew?"

"Not until tonight. About Kellen that is. It's okay, Vanessa. Cian won't hurt us."

"We won't hurt you, Vanessa," I said using a little compulsion. She needed to calm down or we'd never be able to fix what just happened. "Take a seat."

Magdalena kissed me lightly on the lips and said, "Thank you."

"You and Ari should go upstairs to the office and wait. Don't come back down for at least five minutes." She gave me a puzzled look. "Unless you want to forget everything that happened here tonight."

"Oh. Yeah. Okay." She nodded in understanding. Then she turned to her friends, Vanessa and Tanner, who both stood, frozen in shock, mouths gaping, along with the rest of the humans in the club. "I'll be right back," Magdalena whispered and walked up the steps to the office with Ari to wait until we'd cleaned up the mess that the young, jealous werewolf had caused.

"Come on. Time to go back on stage. The Lost Boys have some work to do."

It took a few minutes to get everyone settled down and quieted. I pulled a chair up and sat as though I were about to sing a soft ballad, but instead, I put the guitar down.

"I want everyone to look up here." I'd never tried to compel an entire room of people before. But I had my brothers to help. We all held the trance and managed to capture the undivided attention of every human in the room. It didn't take as long as I'd anticipated with the help of the other three vampires. We were already in the middle of a song by the time Magdalena and Ari came back. I'd practically been holding my breath waiting for the two of them to return. It was difficult to concentrate on anything with Magdalena out of my sight.

Chapter Twenty-Two

Magdalena

I was well into the second month of my new job and loving it. I found it very exciting most of the time, though today my enthusiasm was only half there. I was exhausted from all the nights spent with Cian, and as I examined my ashen complexion, I knew vitamins and protein were not helping my anemic appearance. We were going to need to do something to fix that. If I continued to only give fifty percent to my job, I wouldn't last long in this fast-paced industry, and Josh was relentless. Always needing to be the first at every crime scene.

Getting an inside look into a murder was not only thrilling but very enlightening. Though it was difficult at times when some extraordinary, unexplainable event would take place and I had to wonder exactly what had happened, thinking about Cian and his family and all the other supernatural beings that might be lurking in the city. Speculations and hypotheses that the news and the authorities often surmised shocked me. They had no idea. I would never divulge what Cian and his brothers were, and I knew they were never responsible for any of the crimes, but Cian had told me there were other vampires in the city, most not as nice as he and his brothers. I was getting pretty good at contributing some of my own theories to many of the unexplained events. Sometimes receiving a rolled eye from Josh.

I saw Cian almost every night. I only stayed at his place on Friday and Saturday nights, though. The rest of the time, I came home, since I needed to be up for work early during the week. Cian stayed with me those nights but left hours before the sun rose. Though he had assured me that he never succumbed to bloodlust anymore because he had me and refused to drink from anyone else. But his brothers still did. I had my own ideas of what a vampire did at night, and I was positive that I didn't want to know what Cian's brothers were up to. Though I tried to think of positive things, like maybe they stole blood from hospitals. But that wouldn't be cool either, and I hadn't heard of any blood banks and hospitals being broken into. I supposed it was just as Cian had claimed. That his brothers fed from humans, only taking what they needed to survive and then compelling the victims to forget. But I knew in my heart that was still wrong.

I began to question my sanity. Why did I go along with it all? Why did I continue to see him? Was he compelling me? He'd said he never would, and I had to believe him. My feelings for him were strong and growing stronger every day. Just as the psychic reader Tessa had proclaimed, I had fallen. Fallen deeply in love with a vampire.

I was sitting at my small desk behind the cubicle walls at work, perusing the Internet when Josh walked up behind me.

"Grab your purse. We have a hot one."

I turned around quickly to ask what was up, but Josh had already left my area and was heading out the door. If I didn't hurry, I doubted he would wait. As I followed him into the elevator, catching the door just moments before it closed all the way, I took in my mentor standing beside me, studying his notebook. His dark blue shirt was a wrinkled mess, and his dark hair was tousled in disarray as if he'd just gotten out of bed in a hurry, which he probably had, considering how he hadn't even waited for me to respond before taking off.

"They discovered a woman's body in the Presidio," Josh said, rubbing his day old stubble. Another clue that he'd hurried into work this morning. He was usually well groomed and clean-shaven.

"Oh, no."

"Well, on the grounds of the Presidio. But right now, that's all I know."

When we arrived at the Presidio, they were lifting the body off one of the park benches and placing her into a black zip-up body bag. Her face, covered in blood and claw marks was practically unrecognizable. If she didn't have a driver's license on her, identifying her would be tough. More blood dripped from her neck and arms onto the ground. After they had lifted her into an ambulance, we overheard one of the deputies say that the woman had been left sitting upright on the bench as though she'd been alive and just resting.

"How long has she been dead?" Josh asked one of the officers.

The cop gave Josh a sour look. "You know I can't divulge anything yet, Josh."

"Come on, Detective, you owe me. Besides, you know it's going to be all over the media with false assumptions in about thirty minutes from now if you don't give me something. Give me some facts so I can let the people know the truth."

The officer tucked his notebook inside his uniform breast pocket and glanced around the area. "Okay. But this can't get out for at least another hour. Understand? We need to notify her family first, and I'm heading over there now. I need at least one hour before this hits the air. Do I have your word?"

"You got it." Josh nodded and pulled out his own pad.

"She's been here for a few days, apparently. From what the

coroner said, anyway. Her neck was broken."

"Anything else unusual?"

"Yeah. There were multiple bite marks on various places of her body," the deputy said.

Bite marks? My mind instantly thought of Cian and his band. They couldn't have done this. He swore to me that they never killed. But then, there was also Kellen. As angry as I'm sure he was, being beaten by four vampires, I could just imagine what he might be capable of. He certainly wasn't the man I thought I knew and loved.

"Who was she?" Josh asked.

"We're gonna hold that information until the family has been notified. That's all I can tell you right now. Excuse me," the detective said and stepped away toward another group of cops.

"What do you think?" I asked Josh.

He shrugged. "Could be some sort of cult, making a statement or a sacrifice. Or maybe she was inflicted with those bites prior to someone breaking her neck. Hard to tell at this point since we didn't get a close-up of the body or the bite marks. Those extremists do tend to make an appearance this time of year, though I've never heard of any actual killing before. We're most likely dealing with some sicko who thought it would be funny to emulate fictional vampires or werewolves. Hard to tell which one without seeing the marks." He laughed, but I didn't join in.

I swallowed what felt like a mound of sand lodged between my tonsils. Now that I knew the supernatural world really existed, wasn't just fiction, and was all around us in our everyday lives, I didn't know what to think about this murder.

Josh stood in front of Rex and his camera, recapping everything we'd learned about the murder so far. I stood by, watching. Josh was a pro, and the camera loved him, even as disheveled as he was today. Someday that would be me.

"I'm going to call this in and tell them to air it in an hour,"

Josh said when he was all finished. He headed toward a cluster of trees by another bench.

I walked in the other direction, pulled my own phone out of my purse, and dialed the number that Cian had given me. I just needed to hear his voice, then I'd feel better. It rang several times and went to voicemail. I disconnected the call without saying anything. I wasn't sure how my voice would come across in a message, and I didn't want to alarm him. The time on my phone read 11:33 a.m. He was most likely sleeping. The crazy hours we kept to accommodate each other's lifestyles were murder on us both.

Josh walked up to me. "We might as well get out of here. They're too tight-lipped. We won't find out anything more from them today. Let's go have some lunch."

"Lunch? After visiting a murder scene?" My stomach rolled with disgust. I didn't think I'd be able to eat anything for at least a day or two.

"Come on, we didn't see anything that gory. Just a little blood."

A little blood. I shouldn't be upset about seeing a little blood, but I was pretty shaken up. I'd never seen a dead body before.

"Was that your first?"

I nodded.

"You'll get used to it. Let's go."

Josh and I headed to some small dive for lunch.

"All the locals go here. You'll love it," he promised.

When I caught sight of the joggers and all the people fishing off the pier as we got out of the car, I worried that this local dive, as Josh had called it, would be either a fruit juice bar or a place where all they served were dishes as hideous as raw octopus and mussels. Not something my stomach would be able to handle after seeing that woman's body. I was pleasantly surprised when we entered the National Park of Chrissy Fields, set beneath the Golden Gate Bridge. The view of the bridge from underneath was amazing. It was so intimidating and large from this angle. I handed Josh my phone.

"What's this for?"

"Take my picture with the bridge behind me."

"Really? You want to play tourist?"

I grinned and he snapped the picture, handing me the phone. "Here you go, Mags." The shortening of my name was inevitable as soon as I told anyone it was Magdalena. Josh had called me Mags ever since he first looked at my resume. Even though I had introduced myself as Maggie. Cian was the only one who hadn't shortened my name. Oh, every once in a while he would call me Maggie, but for the most part, I was Magdalena to him.

I took the phone from Josh. The picture he'd just taken was surreal as I gazed upon my giant head against the entire span of the bridge behind me. My eyes instantly went to the first tower where Cian had taken me, the first time he'd drunk my blood. The orgasmic memory made my heart skip a beat. We'd had several of those moments since, but that first one…well, you never forget your first time.

"Pretty nice view, huh?" Josh said, jolting me from my reminiscence. "You should have that new boyfriend of yours take you on a tour of the city. You said he's lived here for a while, right? He should know all the local hangouts."

"Yeah, I'll do that."

Chapter Twenty-Three

Cian

Music permeated the entire mansion, as if someone had turned every speaker of the intercom system on high. Lovely, classical music filled my ears and my mind. I closed my eyes and let the trill of the violin sooth my dark soul. Oh, the memories that came flooding back. I played a lot of rock music these days, but I was a two-hundred-year-old vampire and a sucker for a Tchaikovsky violin Concerto. Lane must have put it on and not realized he had it floating throughout the entire mansion. The blinds were up, which meant I'd slept the entire day after leaving Magdalena.

I had a sudden urge and got out of bed to retrieve my violin. I hadn't played it in years, and now I had an itch to let the bow flow over the strings. Maybe I'd bring it out at the club this coming Saturday. It was always a nice touch to spice up some good rock songs with a violin. We hadn't done it in years. I couldn't remember why.

"Lane!" I yelled, but my excitement halted at the frightening sight, standing in the doorway to my room.

"*Bonjour*, Cian." Jewels' beguiling French accent floated across the room and hit me in my gut.

"Jewels." Her name was the only thing I could utter, the despicable sight of her rendering me speechless.

"That's all you have to say? After all this time, my sweet? No, 'Jewels, it's lovely to see you' or 'I've missed you, where have you been all these years?'" she said, derision coating her tone.

"Nothing so positive comes to mind," I said, finding my voice, and not in the mood to play her disgusting games.

"Ah. I see you've grown some balls over the years." She laughed and skated across the floor toward me.

"How did you get in here?" I asked. I hadn't invited her in.

"Well, I've missed you…and your brother, and I don't need an invitation to enter the home of my children." She skimmed her long, well manicured blood-red fingernails down the side of my face. "Look at this fabulous house you and Lane have. I never doubted your ability to make it without me."

"What do you want, Jewels?"

"Well, I was hoping that we—you, Lane, and I—might reenact the little rendezvous we had that long-ago night on the boat. For old time's sake, of course."

"I don't think so."

"Cian, what the hell is going on with the mus—?" Lane's words were cut off by the sight of Jewels, as I knew they would be.

"Lane, *mon vilain*." She glided over the five large steps to him and kissed him on the lips. He just stood there. "You were always the more eager of the two, you naughty man. Do you remember how you used to beg for more?"

"Get away from him," I barked. "I'll ask you again. How did you get in here?"

"Cian." She turned back to face me, leaving Lane for the moment. "You should know better than anyone how simple it is for a vampire to enter a room without being noticed. I've seen you hovering just inside that sweet young woman's room, watching her sleep. How pathetic you've become. I said to myself, 'Poor, lonely,

Cian. He has needs.' Now, I ask you, who better to tend those needs than *moi*?"

She'd been there those nights I'd watched Magdalena?

"Did you like the artwork? I had it done years ago. But when your pretty little female came into my gallery, I knew she had to have it. To be fully immersed in your world, she'd want to have a family portrait."

She went to the bottle of scotch on the table and poured herself a generous portion.

"Surprised, Cian? Yes, I've been here in the city for over a hundred years. I left briefly after that dreaded earthquake in the early part of the twentieth century. And then they had another one, what, almost thirty years ago, or there about." She flipped her hand in the air in an, it-doesn't-matter-fashion. "If memory serves."

She'd been watching us since the beginning. She'd been there when I'd first spoken to Magdalena in the club that night.

"You leave her out of this."

"Her? The human? Seriously, Cian. You're a vampire. You should never be concerned about a human female. They are here for our pleasure, *non*?"

"No." I shook my head.

"Tsk, tsk. I should not have left you for so long. A mother should stay with her children, *oui*? Then you would be true vampire. I have failed in this respect." She shook her head and then placed her hand on her forehead as if she were truly sorry she'd left us. Then, within seconds, she was centimeters from me, hands squeezing my neck as she shoved me back against the wall. Her once beautiful face was contorted and ugly, fangs protruding from beneath her upper lip. The realization that this was the monster who'd made *us* monsters made me sick, and if I could, I'd have ended it all at that moment. But she was older, stronger.

"You are not to argue with me," she growled. "I am your

maker. Your *maman* so to speak."

"Our mother died many years ago," I coughed out, barely able to understand my own words.

"I am your mother now. I own you and your brother, Cian. Did you think I'd forgotten all about you two? Never! You and Lane are my prize possessions, *mon trésor*."

"It's too late, Jewels. We are not your treasures." Lane yelled. "We don't belong to anyone. We've done very well on our own, as you can see. We don't need you, we never needed you. Let Cian go."

I feared what she would do to Lane for speaking to her that way. We didn't know her at all, didn't know what she was capable of, or what she might do when she was angry.

"Yes, I see that." She smiled and released me. "But alas. I've grown lonely and I need my boys," she pouted.

The quick change in her disposition confused me, and I felt myself slipping back to that boy I'd been so many years ago.

Her dress dropped to the floor and she went to my bed and splayed her naked body out on top. "Lane, come here and kiss me while Cian fucks me."

He took a step toward the bed. "Lane, don't," I said. Lane glanced at me then back at her. I knew he was experiencing the same pulls and doubts as I was, and I tried to fight against her will, no matter how strong the temptation was.

"Oh, I forgot, Lane is the younger one. He does what big brother tells him to do. Even more so now that you are *vampire*. Is that not so, Lane?"

She knew exactly the right thing to say to him. He hated that I had been in the world six and a half minutes longer than him. Though we'd never discussed it, I just knew. I loved my brother.

Jewels sat up, her legs hanging over the side of the bed. Like a string on a puppet, a strong force tugged at my cords as my body began to move involuntarily toward the bed. As I stood next to her, she grabbed my arms and yanked me down next to her. "I'd hoped you'd come on your own. But no worries. This works. Say it, Cian! Say the words I've waited too many years to hear."

"No," I said.

"Lane, be a good brother and come here."

Within a couple of seconds, Lane stood in front of her.

"Let your trousers fall to the floor, Lane."

Lane unbuckled his jeans, his half-hard cock right at the level of her mouth. She had us both in a trance. My brother, whom I'd considered very strong, stood in front of her doing everything Jewels told him to do without her even touching him.

"Make yourself hard and stroke your cock, Lane," Jewels ordered, and he complied.

"Fight it, Lane," I shouted at him, but he ignored me and continued to do just as she'd asked.

"See, Cian, Lane knows what he should be doing." She grabbed Lane's balls in her hands, squeezed, and Lane's body jerked in response. His eyes rolled up then returned, giving off that ever-prevalent silver-rimmed glow we both sported upon sexual arousal as he stroked his cock.

Now, say it, Cian!" she growled and grabbed my cock in one hand and held me to her with the other. I was powerless in her grasp. "Say it!"

"No."

"You are trying my patience, Cian. Lane, come closer and fuck me. Your brother is being an imbecile." She spread her legs wide and Lane thrust his cock into her. I sat helplessly beside them, watching my brother pump into her hard and fast as if he'd been injected with a vial of speed. Jewels' hand reached inside my lounge pants and pumped my cock up and down while my palm kneaded her breast under her commands. As hard as I fought it, I couldn't keep my damn shaft from getting hard and erect. She moaned with exuberance as her fangs dropped again. Jewels hadn't been our first ménage those many years ago, and she certainly hadn't been our last. I'd watched my brother fuck before, and he'd seen me, but never before had we both been helpless and unable to control a situation.

I fought with every brain cell I had not to give her what she wanted. I even thought of Magdalena's beautiful face and how much I never wanted to be with anyone but her. Except Jewels was very strong and powerful. Very sensual. The temptation too overwhelming.

I was no match for her as, *"Mon bijou,"* the awful French term floated from my lips as if they belonged to someone else. *My Jewel* was the English translation, and it was something she had us repeat to her every time we'd fucked her that night on the boat.

"Mon bijou," Lane repeated, his breath quickening with each pump of his cock.

Jewels' fangs were inches from Lane's neck when he was suddenly thrust back and onto the floor. As if a tornado were let loose in the room, Elvis's arms shoved me out of the way, as Gage picked Jewels up by the throat and catapulted her across the room. She got up and growled at Gage, taking that rapacious stance before flashing to him. But Gage, older and stronger, was quicker as the sound of her neck snapping reverberated throughout the room. When her body fell to the floor, I released a heavy, ragged sigh of relief.

"Who the fuck is that?" Gage said, pointing to Jewels' limp, naked body sprawled across the hardwood floor of my bedroom.

Lane sucked in an agonized breath as he pulled up his pants. "Our maker."

"For fuck's sake. She's a powerful one."

"How did you know we were entranced?" I asked.

"Ari followed Lane up here to see what was going on with the music, but he hung back when he heard the female voice." I nodded in understanding. We'd trained Ari to be cautious when an unfamiliar vampire was around.

"I listened for a minute or two and realized what was going on, so I took off to find Gage and Elvis," Ari confirmed.

"Thanks," I patted Ari on the shoulder. "And Gage, Elvis, thanks for coming."

"Yeah, thanks for having our backs, man. Now, let's get rid of the bitch," Lane said.

"How?" I asked. "Anybody ever kill a vampire before?"

"We could stake her," Elvis said matter-of-factly.

"That's so Hollywood, but it might work," Lane said. "Anybody have a fucking piece of wood?"

"No. I'm pretty certain that a plain old wooden stake will not kill her. I've seen it tried before," Gage said.

While we debated on how we could kill Jewels, she moaned. A couple of seconds later, she stood, gathered up her dress, and slid effortlessly into it, pulling the straps over her shoulders. "Boys, boys, boys, you're testing my patience. Bringing in some muscle was against the rules. Lane, Cian, let this just be a warning. You will have me back in your lives." She walked to the doorway, stopped, and turned. The five of us, too astonished to do much of anything else, just stood, gaping at her. "Take care of your pretty little human, Cian," she said and disappeared out the door.

Gage and Elvis hurried to the hallway, Gage shook his head. "She's fast. El, go check the house, make sure she's gone."

"How did she get in here?" Ari asked.

Lane and I looked at each other. "Apparently, a maker doesn't need an invitation to enter the home of their creations," I said, repeating something similar to what Jewels had said.

"That's true," Gage said.

"She threatened Magdalena," I spoke softly, too afraid to utter that sentence too loudly for fear that Jewels would come back into the room and know just how much that would kill me.

"That, or she wants you to turn her," Lane supplied. I knew he didn't like me having such an intimate relationship with a human, but surely he wasn't suggesting I turn Magdalena simply because Jewels had suggested it.

"I do not want or need a robot." I didn't need to mention Chelle's name, but Lane knew exactly what I meant.

"It's not quite like that. Chelle is coming along. She's not bloodlusting for a kill anymore. It's been five months now. I feel comfortable leaving her on her own."

"Except, she wants to be with *you* every fucking minute."

"It's not so bad," Lane said.

"Are you getting off on her?" I asked, incredulity clear in my tone.

"No. Well, not recently. It's hard to avoid, you know? It's not like she's butt ugly."

"Fuck me!"

"Cian, we are vampires," Gage added. "We may not kill to survive like most, but at the end of the day, we lust for sex and blood. And Chelle is...beautiful."

"You, too?"

"No. She won't have me."

Lane laughed. "Not that he hasn't tried for the past five months."

Gage hit Lane on the back of the head. "I'm not bad looking. She just has a thing for the tall and dark," he said, swiping his fingers through his long, dirty blond curls. Gage could be the poster boy for the Santa Cruz boardwalk. All he needed was a surfboard.

"That's true," Elvis said with a smirk.

"That's enough," I said. "We need to figure out how to protect Magdalena."

"You, uh, really love her don't you?" Lane asked.

"Yeah. I do. And I need your help."

"Okay, then. You got it."

Chapter Twenty-Four

Magdalena

When I arrived home from work, Vanessa had the TV on. She and Tanner sat on the sofa, eating something that smelled delicious. I hadn't had much to eat since the few bites of the small salad I'd managed to choke down at the local eatery by the bridge. I'd only been able to handle a few bites before I couldn't eat anymore. I'd watched Josh scarf down a gigantic hamburger stuffed with avocado, bacon, mushrooms, cheese and whatever else was on that concoction, and I'd almost lost the few bites of salad I'd struggled to eat after the murder scene we'd covered. So, by now, I was famished.

"What is that you're eating, it smells divine?"

"Chicken Marsala. Tanner made it. There's more in the kitchen if you'd like some."

"Thanks. I think I will."

"Grab the bottle of red we left on the table on your way back, will you?"

"Sure."

I fixed my plate and grabbed the bottle, along with another glass. We shared everything like food and drink. It had always been that way, even in college we always took care of each other.

I took my plate and sat down on the sofa next to V.

"It's been all over the news," she said in between bites of chicken and green beans.

"What?"

"The murder in the park. How come Josh gets all the glory? I thought you were supposed to be with him on these outings."

"I was. What do you mean?"

Tanner flipped the channel and there was Josh, standing by the murder scene, talking about it on TV.

"I'm still new. Don't worry, I'll get my chance. I couldn't have spoken anyway. I was too choked up about it. It was horrible, V. I almost lost my lunch."

She put her arm around me. "I'm sorry, sweetie, but you picked your profession, and these are the things that you're going to be dealing with on a daily basis."

"Thanks, Mom."

She laughed. "Anytime."

"Hopefully, we won't have a murder every day."

I finished eating and went to my room, leaving Vanessa and Tanner on the sofa. I was exhausted. The murder had me drained. All I wanted to do was take a long, soothing bath and go to bed. I missed Cian, but I didn't think I could stay up late enough tonight to see him. I'd never tried to call him back today. I didn't want to ruin his sleep. I took the phone out of my purse and frowned at the blank screen. No calls. I threw it down on the bed and headed to the bathroom.

I soaked in the tub, closing my eyes, wanting to forget the horrible scene that continued to play in my mind like an eighties Halloween horror movie. Cian's band, they called themselves "The Lost Boys." Why would they pick that name for their band? The vampires in that movie did a lot of killing. Could he have lied to me about that?

I had to believe he told me the truth. He said he'd never lie to me. What sort of relationship could Cian and I have if I always doubted him? I finished soaking and shaved my legs before getting out of the tub. I thought about calling Cian, but I was exhausted. I pulled on my light blue, silky negligee and hopped into bed. He'd show up here sooner or later, I was sure of it. Getting some sleep now was probably a smart thing to do.

I was a light sleeper and started at the soft sound of breathing.

"Cian?" I uttered with a smile, glad he was there. I wanted to talk to him about the murder and get his thoughts. But he didn't answer me. My dark bedroom didn't afford any clues as to who stood in the corner by my window.

"Who's there?"

"Probably your worst nightmare," a female voice whispered, as a woman stepped forward, allowing the moonlight to illuminate her face. It was the face of the woman in our artwork. She grabbed me and pulled me up by my arms, my legs dangling inches from the floor, her dark eyes holding me with her gaze. I couldn't move. I opened my mouth to scream, but I couldn't utter a sound. How had she entered my room? I hadn't invited her in. Had Vanessa?

"When you brought home that portrait of me and so graciously hung it on your wall, you welcomed me into your home. You know, I could kill you now, but I want my boys to watch. I want Cian, in particular, to see as I drain every last drop of blood from that beautiful vein of yours." Her finger traced a sharp trail down the side of my neck, and I almost lost control of my bladder. "If he behaves, maybe I'll let him finish you off. Yes, you are beautiful, and I see why his mind is so clouded with lust for you that he's forgotten who his real lover is."

We were outside, flying through space, time, I couldn't tell, as everything became a blur. Objects whizzed by so fast they were unrecognizable and I threw up in mid-air. We stopped moving at the entrance to a cave. The sound of the ocean roared in my head.

She tossed me into the darkness as if I weighed no more than a few ounces. I tumbled and rolled, and felt something bang against my head. Then everything faded away and I was lost, floating through a cloud.

The sky was pale blue, clouds cotton white. Rays of sunlight flowed down through the atmosphere. It was so beautiful.

Chapter Twenty-Five

Cian

I stood inside Magdalena's room. The bed was empty, and I checked the rest of the house, but there was no sign of her. It was ten o'clock at night. I peeked inside her roommate's bedroom. Two bodies slept, tangled in each other's arms with soft sounds of snoring. Magdalena was gone. My dead heart fell into my stomach as my eyes shot to the painting above the fireplace.

Jewels.

I yanked the portrait off the wall and smashed it against the bricks on the fireplace.

"What is going on?" I turned to see Vanessa, her mouth gaping as she clutched her arms across her chest and over the thin nightgown she wore. "Why did you do that?"

I gazed into her eyes to compel her back to her bed, to forget what she'd just seen, but she held up her hand.

"Don't waste your time. You can't compel me. I know what you are."

I studied her for a couple of seconds, suddenly recognizing the signs. How had I missed them? The clear and red quartz stones used as decorations around the apartment, as well as several other art sculptures and wall hangings, depicting different versions of unicursal hexagrams. The pentagram symbol she wore around her neck that she twisted in her fingers should have given me a clue right away. "You're a witch," I said, understanding.

She nodded.

"Yes. Now that we've established that, why the fuck did you just destroy that beautiful painting? And where is Maggie?"

"I don't know, but my guess is that the monster in this picture has something to do with her disappearance."

"Her disappearance?"

"Yes."

"Who is she?" Vanessa pointed at the torn portrait.

"She's..."

"What's going on, babe?" The groggy male voice stopped me from saying the word I hated more than the monster I'd become.

"Tanner. It's okay. It's Cian." She looked at me and gestured with her head toward Tanner. "Go ahead. It'll work on him."

"Tanner," I said, "Go back to bed. Nothing happened here. You didn't see this."

Tanner turned around and shuffled back to bed.

"So, who is that in the picture?"

"The female is my maker. I have no idea who the male is," I confessed.

"What does she want with Maggie?"

"My guess is; she wants me."

"I'm beginning to get the picture here. Did Maggie tell you about the murder she investigated this morning?"

"No, I haven't talked to her. It's been a hellishly busy fucking evening, and I hadn't realized she'd called until just a bit ago. I came over instead of calling. What sort of murder?"

"It's been all over the news. A dead woman left on a bench, bite marks all over her body, her neck broken. Classic, unexplainable shit. You don't know where Maggie is, do you?"

"No. Does Magdalena know about you?"

"No. It's my family's bloodline and we don't go around announcing it."

"She's your best friend," I countered.

"Best friends have their limits. She didn't tell me about you, either. If you and your boys hadn't beaten Kellen's hairy ass to the ground, I never would have known."

I smiled, glad to learn that Magdalena was true to her word but worried as hell about what Jewels would do to her. I went toward the door to leave. "I need to find Magdalena."

"Wait, maybe I can help."

"How?"

She hurried over to the bookcase, opened a small marble box, and pulled out a crystal shaped with the five points of the pentagram at the top and ending in one point at the bottom. "I should be able to locate her with this."

"Okay. Come on."

"Wait." She went to her room, and a minute later came out wearing some jeans and a black hooded sweatshirt. Then she stepped to the sofa and picked up a flowered scarf. "This is Maggie's. It'll help the amulet mark her location."

I tore out of the apartment like a bullet and headed home with a witch in my arms.

Lane, Gage, Elvis, Ari and Chelle sat lazily about the room. Gage and Elvis looked up from their game of Warcraft as I set Vanessa down in the middle of the room.

"You've brought another human home? Fuck, Cian, what is it with you and these two women?" Lane asked then grinned. "Or did you bring this one for me?"

"Jewels took Magdalena."

"Fuck me," Lane said.

"Do you know where? Did she leave any clues?" Gage asked.

I shook my head. "Nothing."

"I have an idea." Chelle, who'd been sitting on the sofa sipping blood from a plastic bag, gave us a bloodied-tooth grin. "When I want to know where Lane is, I close my eyes and concentrate on his blood running through my body. Doesn't her blood run through yours and Lane's?"

"That only works because you're so new and continue to drink my blood," Lane said.

"Cian, Chelle has a point," Gage said. "Haven't you been drinking from Maggie?"

"Yes. But for some reason, I can't sense her. Something is blocking her scent."

"Why'd you bring her here?" Lane pointed at Vanessa.

"I can help," Vanessa said.

Lane sashayed his body up close to Vanessa's then circled her very still form and sniffed close to her neck.

Lane grinned. "A witch. Hmmm…didn't see that coming."

"Don't beat yourself up about it. I hide it very well," Vanessa said without an ounce of fear on her face.

"You're very sure of yourself, witch, knowing you're in a room full of vampires."

"Lane. Leave her alone. We don't have time for games. Vanessa, come over here." I stood by our felt-covered poker table and spread out a map of the city. Everyone gathered around as Vanessa held her amulet by a black ribbon above the map.

She closed her eyes and uttered something that I didn't think any of us made out. Then she opened her eyes and looked up at us. "Can ya'll hang back a bit? You're cramping my powers."

Everyone took a step back.

"Really? You're gonna need to move back more than that. Just go sit over there and leave me to this." She sat down in the chair at the table.

I had to have faith in this witch. At this point, she was my only hope. Lane and I didn't know what Jewels was really like or what she would do to Magdalena. We'd only had that one night with her so many years ago, but if this evening was any indication of the ruthless, heartless creature she truly was, I feared for Magdalena's life.

I paced the floor from one end to the other, waiting. It seemed like hours had passed since I'd brought this witch back with me.

"Cian, you're going to wear holes in the carpet. Sit down," Lane ordered.

"I can't. We're running out of time." I walked over to the table where Vanessa sat, chanting, the crystal swaying beneath her fingers. "Anything?" I knew the answer.

"If you think distracting me is going to get an answer faster, you're sorely mistaken."

I sighed. "This is ridiculous." I stomped back to the sofa and plopped down between Chelle and Lane then watched the meaningless war take place on the screen as Gage and Elvis battled it out on their X-box controllers. Blood spewed on the screen as a sword hacked off the head of something large and ugly. "Fuck. How can you play this shit?"

"Got her!" Vanessa called out, and we all jumped up and raced to the table. "Right here." She pointed to a spot in the ocean that looked to be five miles off the coast.

"There's nothing there but water," Lane said.

"I know. But there has to be *something* there. Something not showing on this map," Vanessa said. "Do you have a computer?"

"Right over there." I pointed to the large screen on the desk, as well as the assortment of laptop computers and Macs spread out on top. "Take your pick."

She laughed. "Okay. Let's check Google Earth and see what's out there."

"Good idea," Lane said, and we all followed him to the computer center. When Google Earth popped up on the screen,

Lane looked at us. "What should I type in?"

"Try, 'islands off the coast of San Francisco,'" Vanessa said.

The deep blue of the ocean swarmed with small little dots, all representing land.

"There," Gage said, pointing at a dot on the screen. "That dot is at the exact spot on the map where the crystal landed."

Lane slowly moved the mouse, hovering over the dot. "That's the Farallon Islands," Lane read the small description. "It's a group of islands and rocks. Aulon Island, Arch Rock, and others. Also known as the devil's teeth."

"That sounds exciting," Chelle said. "So, when do we go?"

"You don't go anywhere," Lane said.

"What? Why? I can help."

"You're too young, too new to vampirism. You'll get killed," Lane said. "I didn't save you from death just to watch you die at the hands of my maker."

"If I didn't know better, I'd almost believe you guys had real live beating hearts," Vanessa said. "You're certainly not like any other vampires in the city. Hmmm...immortal hearts of San Francisco. That's sort of catchy." She grinned. "Now, go get our girl."

"The islands lie twenty-seven miles outside the Golden Gate Bridge. Jesus, she could be on any one of them," I said.

Chapter Twenty-Six

Magdalena

"Ugh." I moaned. The side of my head hurt, and I tried to raise my hand to touch the spot, but I couldn't move it. I opened my eyes, but everything was fuzzy. I felt the trickle of blood down my temple. Squinting, I tried to gain some focus. It was dark, cold, and the ground I was lying on was wet and sandy. The smell and sound of the ocean were strong. My hands were bound behind my back, and I tried to make out my surroundings, but all I could see was dark walls and a small opening where the sound of the ocean came from. I was in some sort of cave. Then I remembered the woman who had carried me through the sky and I threw up again.

"You're awake." Kellen's voice reverberated with glee from one side of the small space to the other.

"Kellen?" The hoarseness of my voice was thick and I coughed to try and clear it.

"Mags. I told you, you belong to me."

"Kellen? Why am I here?"

Horror swept through my bones. Kellen was behind this. I should have known he'd try something, attempt some sort of retaliation. But I honestly thought that Cian and his brothers had done a good job of discouraging him. I guess I meant more to Kellen than I'd thought.

"Those vampires are scum, Mags. How could you lower yourself to be in collusion with them?"

"Careful, wolf." My head snapped to the sound of a female voice. The one who'd abducted me. "That's my family you're talking about."

Her family?

"Wh...who are you?"

"You don't know? You have my portrait hanging in your home, but you have no idea who I am? I'm crushed that my sons did not tell you."

"Your sons?"

"Cian and Lane, of course."

My head hurt and I was very confused. I squeezed my eyes tightly and tried to make sense of everything. I shivered in the cold, damp spot I sat in, wearing only my thin negligee.

"I don't understand."

"Well, I didn't give birth to their human forms, but I did sire their current vampiric existence."

She'd made them? She was the monster Cian had told me about. The picture was of her. Cian hadn't mentioned that when he'd asked me about it. "What do you want with me?"

"You? Why, I don't want anything with you. But, the wolf here, does. And I suppose you, apparently, are the only thing that will bring Cian to his knees. What he sees in you is beyond me. You have no curves whatsoever, and your hair, darling, you really must start seeing a new stylist."

"Did you kill that woman at the park?"

She shrugged. "A girl's got to eat. And, lucky for you I did, or I'd be sinking my fangs into your neck right now."

"You said you wouldn't hurt her," Kellen snapped.

"Yes, yes I did. That was the deal. Now, let's get this party started." She stood close to me, her breath sweet, like honey. I was almost surprised by that. I'd expected her to have a nasty smell. But she was intoxicating. Her fingers went to my neck, skimmed along the chain of the heart pendant Cian had given me. Then, with one hard yank, she pulled it off me.

I gasped in surprise.

"What are you going to do?" I asked, but she didn't answer. Instead, she took off like a bat out of hell—she must have hit me harder than I thought if I could be joking at time like this—leaving the cave and me alone with Kellen.

"Kellen, why are you helping her?"

"Because, alone, I can't kill that bloodsucker you've been sleeping with. Not as long as he has help from his skanky vamp buddies. But when Jewels approached me with this plan, I figured, why not? Together, we will be able to take the lot of them out. Once we do, you'll be with me again."

I closed my eyes. How in the hell had I ever gotten mixed up with a werewolf and a vampire? It was a harsh reality to realize that the safe world I once knew had never existed. How long had vampires and werewolves been in existence? I didn't think Cian even knew the answer to that.

Chapter Twenty-Seven

Cian

"How about a truce?" Jewels stood by the window of the living room; her red, lacy dress flowed to the floor. She looked every bit the queen of the night that she so desperately wanted to be. Complete with dark, wavy tendrils cascading down her back and her overly plump breasts revealed by the way the gown dipped open to her navel, covering only her nipples.

Gage and Elvis took a stance to attack.

"Keep your goons at bay, Cian. I promise not to compel you or Lane, but you really do need to come with me."

Lane grabbed Chelle and Vanessa by the arms and pulled them across the room as far from Jewels as he could get them.

"Why should I?" I said.

"Well, I know a little secret." She giggled, her fingers grazing her lips as if she were a dainty little debutant.

"What do we care about your secrets?" Lane asked.

"You may not care, Lane. But Cian surely will. You see, I know a certain young, stupid—*very* stupid—werewolf, and I bet he has his filthy paws all over your precious little human right now. As we speak, as a matter of fact."

"Kellen?" Vanessa asked.

Jewels' head snapped up and she hissed at Vanessa. "Another human? No, wait, a witch." She laughed then noticed Ari and flashed in front of him, her face an inch from his. She glided around him and licked the side of his neck. "This one has held my interest for some time now. Such a fine specimen for a human."

Ari, don't move, I told him with my mind. I didn't want him to antagonize her and make her do something rash, like kill him.

"Don't worry, Cian. I won't harm your human slave. In fact, I admire you for possessing him. It takes much discipline on your part not to kill him. I, myself, have never been much for keeping a human around longer than a meal's worth of time. I guess I just don't have the willpower."

"Why should I believe that you, of all vampires, would collude with a werewolf?"

"Because I have this." She continued to lick Ari's neck as she held up the chain with the heart I had given Magdalena, dangling it in the air.

My chest constricted as if a metal vice had clamped tightly around my heart.

"Is that our mother's?" Lane asked.

I nodded slightly at Lane but kept my eyes on Jewels. His question hadn't been one of accusation, more affirmation. It was mine to do with as I pleased. He had his own mementos of our mother.

My teeth clenched and I growled. "I swear, Jewels, you will regret the day you turned us. If you so much as hurt one tiny cell in Magdalena's body..."

She laughed. "You are pitiful."

"What do you want?"

"I want you and Lane to come with me, darling. To be with me. I want you standing by my side, with me as queen of this city, your beloved San Francisco. It's been without a vampire sovereign for too many years now."

"San Francisco is a free territory. It always has been."

"My point, exactly. Which makes it available for the taking, something you should have done a long time ago."

I'd never wanted to rule the city. I loved the way our lives were. Peacefully playing our music weekly. Things had been that way for seventy years, and we had no desire to change it.

"The vampires here are happy the way things are. No one needs to sit in rule and judgment over anyone or anything. Vampire dictatorship has never had a purpose here. What makes you think it's necessary now?"

"Because I said so." Her voice became deep and gravely, as if she'd been demon possessed. Maybe she was. Was that even possible? Maybe that's what had driven her to be what she was. Lane, Gage, Elvis, and I were different. We'd always been the peaceful sort.

"If we do this, you will release Magdalena?"

"What are you saying?" Lane asked.

"Of course, but you may have to fight her greedy young werewolf for her." She laughed a hideous cackle.

The werewolf would need to die if he caused a problem. I lowered my eyes to the floor, unable to look at my brother. "I will come with you and stand by your side."

"As my lover?"

"Yes. But only me. Not Lane." She started to protest. "And *I* will only come if Magdalena is released, not only from you, but from the werewolf, as well."

"That should do," she said. "One brother, I suppose, is better than none. For now."

"You can't be serious," Lane said. "Don't give in to her, Cian. Not for a human."

"Give me a minute to speak with my brother, in private. Then

I will go with you," I said.

"As you wish. You have two minutes. I'll just hold on to this fine human specimen here until you return. And your goons over there had better not get any brilliant ideas, or I will snap this one's neck before they can blink an eye." She stood behind Ari, placing her hands on each side of his head, rubbing her pointy fingernails down the side of his neck.

Lane and I went into the hallway, and he grabbed my shoulders, holding me in front of him. "I know you love Maggie, but this is ludicrous," he said through clenched teeth. "You'll be giving up your freedom."

"A freedom I've had for too many years. I'm tired, Lane. I should be dead. *We* should be dead. We should have died a hundred and fifty years ago, along with our sisters and our parents."

"Yes, you're right, but we're not dead, we're here. We are in this together. I can't bear the thought of you being with Jewels. She will turn your mind against me. You know that."

"I won't let that happen."

"You won't be able to stop it."

"Lane, I have to do this. If she hurts Magdalena, I couldn't bear to be in this life of eternity any longer anyway."

"But Maggie's human. She will die eventually. Then what will you do?"

"At least, this way, Magdalena will live the life she was meant to live, and I can exist, knowing I was not the cause of her death."

Lane pounded his fist into the wall, making a six-inch hole in the plaster. "I don't want you to do this." His voice cracked with the threat of tears. "We started this life together, you and I, in our mother's womb. I don't think I can survive in it without you."

It took a lot for my brother to show so much emotion, and it caught me off guard. I went to him, placed my hand on the back of his neck and pulled him to me until our foreheads met. His eyes glistened with moisture, as did mine.

"You must, Lane. You must survive. I love you. You're my brother. I will always love you. But let me go. In our two hundred years on this Earth, I've never loved another as I do Magdalena. Let me do this for the woman I love."

The Adam's apple in his throat bobbed up then back down as he swallowed and his body stiffened with renewed strength. "We will get you out. If it takes another two hundred years, we will free you from her clutches. I promise."

Chapter Twenty-Eight

Magdalena

The dark, damp cave reeked with the smell of dead fish. If I'd had anything left in my stomach, I would have thrown up again when my eyes fell on a pile of bones heaped in the corner. Could have been human, could have been animal. I didn't want to ask. I didn't want to know.

Snores from Kellen sleeping a few feet away from me echoed off the cave walls, making the sound even more irritating than usual. I'd struggled with the ties secured around my wrists the entire time Kellen slept, trying to wiggle out of them, but had only managed to cut my wrist in the attempt.

I had no idea how long I'd been held there. My spirits brightened when I looked up and saw Cian walk in. "Cian!" My heart leaped and hope soared, but my spirits fell quickly as Jewels' long, curvy figure followed in closely behind him.

"Magdalena!" Cian ran to my side. "Baby, are you okay?"

I nodded. "Now that you're here."

"I'm sorry, Magdalena. I'm so sorry I got you involved in this." He turned to Jewels. "You have what you want, now let her go."

What did she have now?

Jewels stepped over to Kellen and kicked him in the shin. "Wake up, you miserable wolf."

Kellen groaned and sat up quickly when he saw Cian.

"If that wolf lays one finger on her, I'll kill him."

"Likewise, bloodsucker," Kellen growled. "Mags was just a pawn to lure your ugly ass here, you stupid fuck. She belongs to me. And you belong to her." He motioned to Jewels. "*Your* master. You always have. Isn't that the way of the skanks?"

"You're one to talk, wolf. Where's your fucking pack? You weren't wolf enough to claim Magdalena, that's why you haven't, and your pack knows it. Yet you continue to act as if you have. You can't keep her prisoner until you've reached maturity. You live in a fucking dream world, pup."

"Boys! Stop this annoyingly childish banter," Jewels shouted, and my head began to swim with all the information that Cian and Kellen had just dumped at each other.

"Cian, what did he mean?" He ignored my question, but I already knew what Kellen had been talking about. "You're not going to stay with her, Cian." I couldn't believe that he would make that deal with her. "You can't give yourself to her. Please, don't."

He gently brushed a strand of my hair away from my face and tucked it behind my ear before skimming his thumb over my lips. "I have to do this. You deserve to live a full life. If you'd never met me, your life would not be in danger right now. You wouldn't even be here. You'll never be safe with me in the hell I live in."

"Please, Cian, don't." My vision blurred from the tears welling in my eyes.

"It's too late, he's already made his decision," Jewels barked out and walked behind me, breaking the zip strips that secured my wrists with a slice of her razor-sharp nails. "See, my love? I kept my word. She is free to go. That is if she can get past the wolf and the ocean back to the mainland."

Cian helped me to stand. "You lied to me, Jewels. You said you would let her go, not that you would release her into the arms of the wolf or to the perils of the sea."

"She is free to go. But I have no control over what happens to her now. She is no longer my concern." She clicked her thumb against her finger as if she were flicking dirt from under one of those wretched nails.

"She is if you want *me* to stay with you," Cian growled through clenched teeth.

Kellen grabbed me and pulled me against him. I pounded my fists into his chest to let me go, to no avail.

Growls reverberated throughout the cave as Lane, Gage, and Elvis stood just inside the entrance. Lane held some sort of blade in his hand. "Let her go, you giant flea bag."

"I believe that was slimeball," Cian said and winked at me.

"So nice of your brother and your goons to join us, Cian. How fun it will be to watch you rip their heads off."

"You can't make me do that," Cian said. "You weren't able to compel me to fuck you, what makes you think you can get me to kill my brothers?"

"Oh, but you were on the edge, Cian, my love. You were definitely on the edge," Jewels crooned out with a seductive grin.

More, deeper growls joined in from over by the cave entrance. Two black wolves took a threatening stance, ready to pounce. Kellen threw me down, and I skinned my knee on a rock as my arm landed against another. Pain seared through my wrist, and bile rose to my throat at the sight of my hand dangling from my arm at an awkward angle.

"You asked about my pack. Well, you should know I'd never try something like this without some of them," Kellen growled then leaped at Cian as the other two werewolves attacked Lane, Gage, and Elvis. I'd seen them all fight—four vampires against one wolf—and win, but I didn't think the three vampires had much of a chance against two huge werewolves that seemed a lot stronger and faster than Kellen.

Tears stung my eyes as I fought past the pain, only to see Kellen's claws break through the skin of his knuckles as he dove at Cian, slicing four large gashes across Cian's chest.

A few feet away, the two wolves snarled and bared their fangs, then the vampires growled, showing their own set of sharp teeth before attacking the wolves. Bodies went flying and fur flew through the air in clumps. Howls and snaps smothered the sounds of the ocean outside.

One of the wolves howled as a blade pierced its side and it fell to the cold, damp ground.

Lane took a running leap and latched on to Kellen's neck, hanging onto his back, biting. Cian punched Kellen right in his elongated, wolf-snouted face, sending Kellen and Lane to the floor in a heap. Lane groaned and scrambled to release himself from under Kellen's massive body as Cian reached out and tugged his brother to his feet.

Both Gage and Elvis tackled the other black wolf; biting its neck until it, too, fell.

Everything was happening so fast around me; I had a difficult time keeping track of it all.

After Lane had gotten to his feet, Cian lunged for Kellen, striking, punching at his jowls over and over again, as if they were ordinary men having a fistfight when he could have simply taken him down by the jugular and let him bleed out. That was when I knew what kind of man, what kind of *vampire* Cian really was. And I loved him even more.

Cian honestly hated killing, even if it was in self-defense. Kellen shoved Cian off of him and scrambled to his feet.

Jewels grabbed me and yanked me from the floor. In all the

commotion, I'd forgotten about her. The self-defense classes my father had insisted I take when I went away to college flooded my mind, and I swung my elbow backwards, catching Jewels in the stomach. The pain from my broken wrist made me want to throw up. *Fight, fight, don't let her overpower you.* She twisted my arm hard behind me and squeezed me so tightly I couldn't breathe. The searing pain from my wrist made me break out in a cold sweat and caused spots to obscure my vision for a moment. I clawed at Jewels from behind me with my free, uninjured arm. Taking note of where her face was, I slammed my head back against hers. I heard the crunch of bone and knew that I'd broken her nose. She let go of me. "You bitch!" she shouted. I stumbled, fell to the ground, and scrambled a few feet away. But not far enough.

Jewels grabbed me by my hair and dragged me back up. I was no match for her vampire strength.

"Cian, stop this fighting, right now, or she dies!" Jewels shouted as she held the sharp blade that Lane had brought into the cave against my neck, her arm securely around my shoulders.

Everyone stopped fighting and stared at Jewels as she held me. Then she laughed a vile cackle. "Here, Cian, I believe this belongs to you." She tossed the necklace Cian had given me to him, and as he caught it, I felt the slice across the front of my neck.

I barely heard Cian scream, "No!" as I fought for air. But none came, and I felt myself falling, falling, falling.

Chapter Twenty-Nine

Cian

The wolf howled in my ear as I watched Magdalena slink to the ground, blood oozing from her neck. Her once beautiful peach-colored skin turning pale before my eyes. I ran to her, tugged off my shirt and pushed it into the wound, pressing, pressing, trying to keep the blood from leaving my beloved's body.

"Magdalena. Baby, hold on. Hold on." I knew it was too late for her. She was dying. I stroked her hair. Her eyes opened.

"Look at me. Don't go. I love you too much, don't leave me."

Jewels' laughter behind me reverberated off the walls of the small cave. I stroked Magdalena's head and my fingers grazed the knife that had sliced her throat. Wrapping my fingers around the white, marble handle, I stood. Jewels continued to laugh, holding her stomach as if the fake, uncontrollable cackle she emitted actually hurt.

"There will never be another for me in this eternal hell, you fucking bitch!" I shouted and shoved the blade hard into Jewels' heart.

Her eyes bugged. "Stupid boy, you know you can't kill..." Apparent pain seized her, and she screamed and fell to the ground.

I wasn't quite sure what had just happened. I knew the knife

I'd jabbed into Jewels wouldn't kill her. But there she laid, her chest still as a corpse.

"Maggie's dead. She killed her. The bitch killed her. This has all been for nothing," Kellen uttered. He let out a deafening howl before running out of the cave. The other two wolves hobbled after him.

I went back to Magdalena's side, crouching on my knees, I picked up the bloody t-shirt and once again tried to stop the bleeding. So much blood. No human could survive that slice. I scored my wrist with my fangs and held my arm to Magdalena's lips. But she remained still. Unresponsive.

"Please, Magdalena, drink a little, just a little to heal the wound. Please, baby, suck a little." I dabbed my finger into my blood and stuck it in her mouth, rubbing it over her tongue and gums. I repeated the act, several times, then put my wrist back to her lips. Still nothing. There was no breath coming from her mouth, and her heartbeat was so faint, if it beat at all, I couldn't hear it. I continued to stick my bloodied finger in her mouth, adding another. Then after several minutes, I felt the tip of her tongue move slightly and she swallowed. I held my wrist over her lips again, parting them with my fingers, letting blood drip into her mouth. Then her tongue slipped out and touched my wrist. "That's it, baby, now suck a little. I know you can. I've felt you."

She began, gentle pulsating pulls. Her heartbeat picked up and the skin on her neck began to slowly knit together until the gash was completely healed. Her pulse became stronger, and I exhaled a sigh of relief.

"That's it. Take more."

I wiped tears from my cheeks. "I'm so sorry, baby, I'm so sorry. I never wanted to turn you. Not this way." Though I knew, eventually, I'd need to make a decision. Turn her while she was still young and beautiful or watch her grow old and die. The latter was not an option.

Her eyes closed and she fell unconscious. I pulled my wrist away. I'd already ingested her blood, she was in my soul, and now, when she woke, I would be in hers.

She would be *vampire*.

Jewels lay on the cold, wet ground of the cave. "Is she dead?" I asked, knowing that was ridiculous. A small blade like that could never kill a vampire.

"No, she's not dead. But she will remain in that deadened state as long as the poison on the blade stays in her system, thanks to Maggie's witch, Vanessa," Lane beamed. "She put a spell on the blade to render her completely paralyzed."

"Long enough for us to take her far away and secure her in chains for the rest of her life," Elvis added.

"We'll take care of Jewels. You get Maggie home. She's gonna be pissed when she wakes up as a vampire," Lane said.

I released a heavy sigh laden with guilt. "I know." I gathered Magdalena in my arms and headed back to the mansion.

Ari was there, waiting, along with Vanessa and Chelle. It had taken Chelle five months just to get to the point where she wasn't begging to be released from her chains to go out and kill for food, to be satisfied to take just enough to survive. Lane still carried extra blood with him whenever he took her out to feed, just in case. I wondered how long it would take Magdalena. Though, Lane only allowed Chelle to drink from him occasionally, now, as he never wanted that type of relationship with her. Turning her had been an accident. But with Magdalena, I knew it had to be this way sooner or later. But I had wanted it to be on her terms. I didn't want a puppet. Magdalena had a mind of her own, and just like Lane and me, she would learn to use it to her advantage. As vampire.

I took Magdalena upstairs and placed her on my bed. I pulled up a chair and watched her sleep. I had no idea how long it would take for her to wake up, but I wanted to be the first thing she saw when she did. I knew it could be days, but I sat and waited. Every so often, Lane would come in and check to see if I wanted anything.

There was nothing that I wanted, except for my lover to wake up.

I lost track of time. I heard the shades rise and lower a couple of times, so I assumed maybe two or three days had passed, but I never moved from her side, not once. Not for sustenance, not for thirst. There was nothing that I needed, except to be right there to feed her more blood as soon as she woke. If I didn't, she would die. When Lane and I had awakened, we'd been forced to kill immediately. I didn't want Magdalena to ever be forced to kill someone for blood. She'd learn. She would want to, I was sure of it.

I sat and watched her and smiled when her eyes moved beneath her lids. Her eyes flashed open as if something had startled her. Her silver-rimmed blue irises shone; my blood clearly in her veins.

"Cian," she whispered as if the act of talking hurt.

"Magdalena, sweetheart. I'm here."

"It hurts."

"Shhhh." I scored a gash along my wrist and held it to her mouth. "Drink."

She shook her head.

"Magdalena, you must drink or you will die."

"No. I don't want to be a vampire."

"Please, my love. Please drink. I can't lose you now. I love you, Magdalena. I fell in love with you the first time I saw you sitting at that restaurant when our eyes first met. I never believed in love at first sight. Not before that night. I don't say this lightly. I've never told another woman that I love her. I will never hurt you."

"No. Can't. I don't want this life, Cian. I love you. I do. I will always love you, and I will love you in the afterlife, wherever that may be, but you should let me die. You had no right to bring me back. You should have left me to die in that cave."

She turned her head, refusing my wrist. I had to convince her to drink my blood or she would die. The sleep rendering us immobile shortly after ingesting vampire blood for the first time is much like death itself. Drinking immediately after waking from that death-enabled slumber was essential for our survival.

Several hours passed as I watched Magdalena fight the urge to take my vein. The immense amount of pain she was experiencing grew stronger and her breaths grew more shallow with each passing minute. She needed to take my blood now, or I feared I'd lose her. "Please Magdalena, I beg you. Please take my blood."

"No. Let me die. Just please, let me die."

"If I do that, then I should have just shoved that poisonous blade into my own black heart because I could never survive an eternity without you."

She squeezed her eyes shut then opened them.

"Please, baby, drink from me. Be strong. Spend eternity with me."

I pressed my wrist against her lips and waited. Maybe she was just too exhausted from the agony that the transition caused, or maybe something I said clicked in her mind. Whatever it was, relief swamped me when her tongue licked my arm before she gently suckled at my wrist.

My blood gave her the added strength she needed, and allowed her to become coherent enough to suckle at my wrist. She would also need to ingest human blood to complete her transition to vampire, but I had a bag at the ready, waiting for her to accept her fate. Rejuvenation after that took only a matter of minutes. Thirty minutes later, Magdalena stood, facing the closed blinds and hugging her arms around her midriff. The sad look on her face practically killed me. I understood the weight of that expression—the knowledge that you will never be able to look upon the sun again or feel its rays upon your skin heavy in your mind.

"How will I do this, Cian? How do I tell my best friend and the closest thing to family that I have left that I'm a vampire?"

"The same way your best friend's going to tell you that she's a witch," Vanessa said from across the room. I'd mentally sent Lane to get her as soon as I knew Magdalena was taking my blood.

Magdalena turned to watch her friend cross the room. "V? You're here?"

"Yeah, I'm here." They ran to each other and embraced.

"What did you just say?" Magdalena asked.

"I said I'm a witch. I've always been a witch. My mother is a witch. I knew Cian and his brothers were vampires since the night Kellen came into the bar and attacked them. I can't be compelled."

"So you pretended."

Vanessa nodded.

"Why didn't you tell me?"

"Same reason you didn't tell me about your boyfriend being a vampire. There are just some things you don't reveal until the time is right."

Magdalena looked around the room at everyone standing by, watching and waiting to see what would happen.

"What happened to Jewels and Kellen?" Magdalena asked.

"I came up with a spell that would make a knife poisonous to a vampire," Vanessa said. "The plan was for someone to stick Jewels with it, thus paralyzing her long enough to be dealt with."

"Cian stabbed her. But he didn't know the blade was poisoned at the time," Lane said.

"It was purely blind rage," I admitted. "I was so fraught with anger about her slitting your throat, I grabbed the first thing I saw that would inflict pain upon her in any way."

"She's securely chained inside a metal box. Lane thought of

the chains and the box. I came up with the remote island off the coast of New Zealand," Gage said. "I happened to know of a great spot where no one will ever disturb her. Not only is she in chains inside a metal box, but we also lowered it down to a ledge inside a volcano. She'll burn to death if she ever happens to get out of the chains and the steel container."

"After the witch had said she could put a spell on the blade, I came up with the idea of the box and the volcano from Cian's threat to me the other day," Lane admitted.

I grinned. "You know I would never have done that to you."

He nodded. "Yeah. But you were quite convincing at the time."

"What about Kellen?" I asked.

"He took off after you beat the crap out of him and then stabbed Jewels." Lane turned to Magdalena. "He thinks you're dead, Maggie."

"I remember watching you fight Kellen," Magdalena said to me. "You were fist-fighting like humans." A small smile graced her face.

"I'm glad you're okay, Mags," Vanessa said. "That would have sucked if you died. No pun intended. Vampire or not, I'm glad you're here."

They embraced again, but I had to pull Magdalena away from her friend when her fangs elongated and she looked about to sink them into the side of Vanessa's neck.

"I'm sorry," Magdalena said, covering her mouth with her hand.

"I get it. Listen," Vanessa said, taking several steps toward the door. "I'm going to go now. Call me when you're able to be around humans again."

Everyone else left along with Vanessa, and Magdalena stood in front of the window staring at the cream toned iron shades.

"You've made me into a monster," she whispered.

"You could never be a monster." I came up to stand beside her. "It was inevitable, Magdalena. Sooner or later, I knew I'd need to turn you. I just…I just wanted it to be your decision, not Jewels' or anyone else's. Would my eternal fate in hell without you have been better than a life with you as my mate? Would you have subjected me to that, Magdalena?"

Chapter Thirty

Magdalena

I didn't know what to say to Cian. He'd left me alone for a while, and even after thinking about it more, I still didn't know what to say. I did love him, and no, I wouldn't have wanted him to spend eternity without me if it would hurt him, but I hadn't really had time to process the idea. To think any of this through.

We sat in his room. The shades had gone up and it was a beautiful night as I watched the lights on the bridge. Cian came up beside me and wrapped his strong arms around me.

"Are you okay?" he asked.

"Cian, I just…well, I'd never considered being a vampire. I just thought I'd spend my life with you as a human. Grow old and die a normal human death whenever and however that occurred."

"I'd rather be staked in the heart a thousand times over than watch you grow old and die."

I stared at him as the lightbulb in my head went off. "We really can't die?"

"No. That's not completely true. We can die. If we are decapitated or burned in fire, we will perish. But if one manages to avoid that nasty demise, we will never grow old, never get fat, and never get grey hair or wrinkles."

I wanted to see what I looked like, but Cian didn't have any mirrors that I knew of. "Do I look any differently?"

"You're more beautiful, which I never thought possible."

"I wish I could see my face."

"You can."

"But I thought…there are no mirrors here."

He shook his head. "No. There are not. Come here." He pulled me close to him. "Look into my eyes." I did. "Do you see your reflection?"

"Yes, but that's not very large."

He smiled and took me to the computer and turned it off. There we were, standing side by side in the reflection of the dark computer screen. "This is the best I can give you."

"Why can't we see ourselves in a regular mirror?"

"That puzzled me for years. But from what I understand, a mirror requires radiant light to reflect an image. Radiant light comes from sunlight. We, as vampires, cannot stay in direct sunlight without having all of our energy drained from us, so we don't have enough radiant light in us to generate a reflection in a mirror."

I decided it wasn't worth dwelling on my appearance. I was a fucking vampire. What did I care how I looked? Besides, every vampire I'd met so far had been beautiful. Cian, Lane, Chelle, all of them. Even Jewels was gorgeous to the point of obnoxiousness. I've never hated anyone more. Cian's maker or not, she was a monster and he should have killed her.

"Cian. Why didn't you kill Jewels? Why did you leave her in that state?"

"Death would have been too good for her. This way, she can never hurt or turn another person, but she doesn't get the luxury of eternal rest either. From what the others told me earlier before I came back in to check on you, the poison had paralyzed her body long enough for them to bind her, but her mind was still functioning. *Is* still functioning. At least from what Vanessa said about the spell. That's got to be hell, to know you are chained up inside a metal box and can't get out, feeling the suffocating heat of the volcano around you."

He reached into his pocket and pulled out the necklace he'd given me.

"Here, I think this belongs to you," Cian said as he placed the gold heart pendant around my neck.

"You caught it. I remember."

"Yes, and ever since, I've ached to put it back on you."

I fingered the delicate heart that had his name etched on it. It was so pretty. My soul overflowed with elation, so proud that he wanted me to wear something so special to him.

Cian gently tugged me against him. Lifting my chin with his finger so that our lips were just inches apart, he kissed me. Tender. Then harder. I wanted more. I wanted him to rock my world the way he'd done the first time he drank my blood. I wanted to know what it would be like now that I'd been turned.

His kiss seared with heat and made every inch of my body tremble with desire. The temptation to tear off his clothes and then sink my teeth into his vein was very strong. I ached to rub my naked body all over his. I kissed him back, wild desperation taking control of every cell in my body. My senses heightened and I detected the vampiric pheromones.

Intoxicating.

Then there was a sudden jolt and the entire room bounced and juggled. At first I thought, *holy hell, Cian read my mind and he's literally rocking my world.* It was magnificent. But then his voice became demanding, forceful as he tugged me over to the doorway of the bedroom.

"We need to take cover. It's an earthquake."

A fleeting notion ran through my mind. *But we are invincible.*

The shaking and rumbling stopped almost as soon as it had started. Nothing in the room seemed out of place nor was anything jostled to the floor from any of the vibrations.

"It was just a small tremor," I said.

"Can't live in San Francisco without having one of those every now and again," he laughed and pulled me back into his embrace.

"What was the point of taking cover if we can't die?" I asked.

"Pain still hurts, even for the short time it would take for you to heal. I didn't want you to feel pain."

Chapter Thirty-One

Cian

"So, what do we do for the rest of eternity?" Magdalena asked.

I pulled her in close so that her chest was against mine, delighting in the slight pressure of her breasts.

"A hobby would be good to have." I grinned.

"Humph. You mean like knitting or something?"

"If you like. You can do whatever you desire. You can take up skydiving if you want."

"That is tempting." She laughed. "What about my job?"

"I think it would be best if you quit that."

"But I just started." The slight pucker of her mouth made my cock twitch, and I wanted to suck on that pouty bottom lip. "It's always been my dream job. That's what I went to school for."

"Quit for now," I added, quelling her protests. "Human contact right now is going to be a bit of a challenge for you. But once you overcome the temptation to kill every human being you come in contact with, well, then you can go back to work. If that's what you want."

"How long will I want to kill?"

I thought about that for a moment. "Do you...*want* to kill someone?" I asked.

"No. But you said…"

"Magdalena. The only reason a vampire kills is for nourishment. We need to ingest human blood to survive. New vampires, when left to fend for themselves like Lane and I were, or others that are raised by animalistic vampires, don't know how to control the urge. They want to drain a body of all of its blood, and therefore, end up killing. They don't mean to do it. Not at first."

"But then, over time, and because of habit, the monster side takes over and that's what they find thrilling," she quipped.

"Something like that." I grinned. "But, Magdalena, you don't need to work if you don't want to. I mean, we don't need the money. *You* won't need the money."

"You expect me to simply live here and not contribute anything?"

"I never said that."

"Then what are you saying?"

"Just that you won't need to work for a living. We have plenty of money, but you can work if you want to, or you can pursue something else entirely. You will have an eternity to experience a multitude of different adventures. And, we will do many of them together. Come here." I led her to the bed. "You haven't had the pleasure of experiencing one of the best parts about being a vampire."

"Are you trying to tempt me into having sex with you?"

"Absolutely."

Her lips curved. Sexy. Seductive.

She placed her palm on my bare chest and shoved me down to the bed. My cock pointed up at her, tenting the loose-fitting lounge pants I wore. But those became nothing more than a memory as Magdalena ripped them from my body. She gasped at her actions. "Sorry. I guess I don't know my own strength."

"I have another pair," I huffed, unable to control my lust. I yanked her down on top of me. I took one of her nipples into my mouth, sucked and scraped my fangs over the little nub as it hardened, making her hips buck at the sensation. My eager hands were already searching up her thighs, and I got rid of her undergarments the same way she had my lounge pants. "You should just stop wearing those, my love."

"Okay," she breathed before lowing herself onto me.

She was so tight. The sensation of her walls hugging my hard shaft stole my breath and I hissed. "Magdalena, I love you. Forever."

"I love you, Cian DeMarco. For eternity."

"Take my vein," I told her.

Her eyes shot to mine. She hadn't taken blood from my neck before. In fact, she hadn't ingested any blood for about four hours. She smiled, her fangs already lowered with anticipation. She placed her mouth to my neck and sank her fangs in. Deep. Sucking as if she'd been doing it for years. And when she positioned herself so that I could also take her vein, I bit into her neck. Her hips bucked up then plunged back down, hard. She grew stronger each time she drank from me.

She raised her head for a moment and screamed, "Cian!" as her sex clenched tightly around me in waves of pleasurable orgasmic ecstasy. She was experiencing a climax of tsunamic proportions, and I let myself fill her with everything I had to give—my essence, my blood, and my love.

Acknowledgments

Many, many thanks to my husband, the love of my life, for giving me the support and opportunity to do what I love and for reading everything I write. I'd be lost without your helpful suggestions. I also appreciate your mentioning my book to every complete stranger you meet, which embarrasses the heck out of me, but I love it and love you. You are my rock and my knight in shining armor. To my kids, for all your love and support and my Mom, for your encouragement and support.

Thank you, Michelle, my outstanding editor, you are the best. You've been a huge help in bringing this book to life with all your encouraging words and praises, along with all the giggles we had at some of the comments. Your tenacity in wanting to make this the best book I've written so far and your drive in pushing me to show more of myself were very much appreciated. I love the way you allow me to pick your brain even when you're probably too exhausted to think. Thank you, to my beta readers Amber Garza, Suzan Lacey, Heidi Hudson, Kimberly Shaw, Trallee Mendonca, Tina Donnelly, Ravannah Rayne, Julie Bromley, Katherine Eccleson, and Amanda Catoe. Thank you for your insightful suggestions, your help in pulling this book together has been remarkable.

Thank you for reading *Tempted by a Vampire*, the first book in the Immortal Hearts of San Francisco series. Writing this story has been one of the most enjoyable endeavors I've ever had the pleasure of undertaking. I live about two hours from San Francisco, give or take a few depending on traffic, and have always been in love with the romance of the city. I've always thought the city would be a great location and setting for a romantic vampire series, and that's how I came up with the idea for Immortal Hearts of San Francisco. I hope you all enjoy Cian's and

Magdalena's story and continue with future stories of all the other characters. I'm hoping to make all the books stand-alones, giving each character their individual spotlight, but sometimes things cross over and bits of information is needed from a prior book, but not enough to ruin the story either way. But if you're a stickler for reading things in order, then I guess that's always the best thing to do.

So, here are some of my future plans...

I'm already working the next book in the Immortal Hearts of San Francisco, but I'm still trying to figure out whose book it is going to be. So, I'm still in the planning stage for that one.

I am one third of the way into the next Beaumont Brothers book, Beautifully Pulled—it's a working title and may change—but it's coming along fairly well. What? You say. A third book in a series that only had two brothers? How is that possible? Well, I'm not going to give anything away just yet, and I don't like to mention character names this early in the writing, because as I get to know them better, sometimes their name changes to suit them better.

As long as we are on the subject of what's coming soon, there is another book in the Sectorium series that I've started. It will be Quinn's book as a grown up and will revolve around her love life as she struggles to cope with her abilities, which if you read Whisper Cape, know that there are probably quite a few.

I always have new ideas popping into my head so there will always be stories coming, both new and continued.

Thank you so much for reading *Tempted by a Vampire* and for spending time with me.

I love you,
Susan

About The Author

Susan Griscom writes paranormal and contemporary romance. She's hooked on gritty romances and is a huge fan of superheroes and bad boys confronted with extraordinary forces of nature, powers, and abilities beyond the norm mixed with steamy romance, of course.

She loves those days when she gets to sit around in her sweat pants, doing nothing but writing emotionally charged stories about love and violence and drinking coffee.

She lives in Northern California with her romantic husband and together they have five great superhero kids and eight mini-superhero grand kids, so far.

Made in the USA
Charleston, SC
18 January 2016